"Don't pity me, Jason. I don't want it,"
Laura said fiercely. "No 'poor little Laura'
from you. I won't have it."

"Under that quiet exterior, you're a tough little cookie, aren't you?" he said, challenging her.

"Yes, I'm tough," Laura said, glaring at him. A strange recklessness poured through her, invigorating her, infusing her with a dizzying exhilaration she had never before experienced. She'd never fought with anyone before. For once she was saying exactly what she felt. "I'm strong, and I always have been. And I don't want—"

" 'I don't want, I don't need,' " Jason mimicked her. "Baby, you're too tightly strung to know what you want or need."

A feverish wildness filled her, and eyes glittered. "Oh, and I suppose you do. Know what I want? What I need?" She was daring him, taunting him, inviting him—and he could not resist responding.

"This is what you want," he said, fastening his hands around her hips and pulling her to him. She could feel his heat, his hunger echoing hers. "This is what you need. . . ."

WHAT ARE *LOVESWEPT* ROMANCES?

They are stories of true romance and touching emotion. We believe those two very important ingredients are constants in our highly sensual and very believable stories in the *LOVESWEPT* line. Our goal is to give you, the reader, stories of consistently high quality that may sometimes make you laugh, sometimes make you cry, but are always fresh and creative and contain many delightful surprises within their pages.

Most romance fans read an enormous number of books. Those they truly love, they keep. Others may be traded with friends and soon forgotten. We hope that each *LOVESWEPT* romance will be a treasure—a "keeper." We will always try to publish

LOVE STORIES YOU'LL NEVER FORGET
BY AUTHORS YOU'LL ALWAYS REMEMBER

The Editors

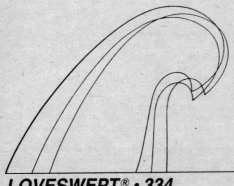

LOVESWEPT® • 334

Barbara Boswell
Simply Irresistible

 BANTAM BOOKS
NEW YORK • TORONTO • LONDON • SYDNEY • AUCKLAND

SIMPLY IRRESISTIBLE
A Bantam Book / June 1989

If you would be interested in receiving protective vinyl
covers for your Loveswept books, please write to this address
for information:

Loveswept
Bantam Books
P.O. Box 985
Hicksville, NY 11802

ISBN 0-553-21998-7

Published simultaneously in the United States and Canada

Bantam Books are published by Bantam Books, a division
of Bantam Doubleday Dell Publishing Group, Inc. Its trademark, consisting of the words "Bantam Books" and the
portrayal of a rooster, is Registered in U.S. Patent and
Trademark Office and in other countries. Marca Registrada.
Bantam Books, 666 Fifth Avenue, New York, New York 10103.

One

It was past four o'clock on the Saturday before Labor Day when Dr. Jason Fletcher arrived at Rock Creek Park for the annual Hospital Center picnic. Members of the food committee, in the midst of preparing the huge dinner for hospital personnel, family members, and friends invited to the picnic, greeted him heartily.

"Fletcher, so you're finally back from Ireland, are you?"

"We want a complete rundown on all those gorgeous Irish colleens, Fletch."

"You're just in time for the softball game, Jason. We knew you'd never miss it."

"Get on over to the game, Fletcher. You're on Flynn's team. He chose you in absentia—and he's going to need you to win this year. Zane Montrose is on the other team and they look unbeatable."

Fletcher frowned. "Unbeatable?" That particular word had always been unacceptable to him, unless applied to himself, of course. Jason Fletcher liked to win, to triumph—and usually did. He considered it both his due and his destiny.

"Zane managed to get almost every nurse who

knows how to hit or field on his team," a red-haired occupational therapist told Jason while she mixed a mountain of cole slaw. "Looks like this is the year you finally lose the big game, Fletcher. It's about time, too." There was a gleefully malicious glint in her eye.

"Sorry to disappoint you, honey, but I never lose," Jason said coolly.

"You're not the least bit sorry to disappoint me," the redhead retorted. "You take great pleasure in disappointing—"

Jason moved away from her fast. Obviously, she was still carrying a grudge against him for ending their brief relationship when she would've preferred it to continue right down the aisle into the steel jaws of matrimony. But to extend that grudge into hoping his team would lose the big game . . .

Jason was appalled. That was not sportsmanlike at all!

The challenge of the game—and the determination to hang onto his unbroken winning streak—sent him racing over to the field where an enthusiastic crowd was cheering wildly for the two competing softball teams. Jason felt his jet-lag fatigue lift. He'd been right to come here directly from the airport, despite the long flight. He loved the annual picnic and softball game and the fact that whatever team he pitched for inevitably won.

Casey Flynn, the Hospital Center's premier trauma surgeon and Fletcher's longtime friend, was at bat. Zane Montrose, first-year orthopedic resident, was pitching for the opposing team.

"Jason! You're here!" Casey's wife, Sharla Shakarian Flynn, also a Hospital Center physician, greeted him with a welcoming smile. "And just in the nick of time too. The game started fifteen minutes ago and the score is six—zero. *Their* favor."

"Strike two!" shouted the umpire, a burly hematologist.

"Case has two strikes on him?" Jason was aghast. It was unheard of. Next to himself, Casey Flynn was the best hitter in the Hospital Center.

"Zane was the pitcher of his college baseball team," Sharla said. "He's very good."

"You're certainly taking this calmly enough," Jason said disapprovingly. Sharla seemed far more concerned with holding her wriggling two-year-old daughter Shannon in her arms than with the unthinkable prospect of her husband's striking out! "You're not on our team, are you?" he asked warily.

He liked Sharla. He always had. She was married to one of his best friends. She was an exemplary wife and mother and a world-class neonatologist . . . but she couldn't play softball worth a damn. Her hitting was awful and her fielding even worse. Jason sometimes pondered Case's ability to overlook these flaws in his wife. He knew that he himself could never love anyone who couldn't even make a baseline hit.

"Don't worry, Jason, I'm not playing this year," Sharla said dryly. Her dark eyes shone with amusement, revealing to Jason that she knew exactly what he was thinking.

"Strike three!" bellowed the umpire dramatically, and a deafening round of mixed boos and cheers followed.

Jason was thunderstruck. "I can't believe it! Montrose struck him out! This is our twelfth annual softball game and it's the first time Case has ever struck out!"

"You look as if your life is passing before your eyes," Sharla observed wryly. "It's just a game, Jason. There's a tried and true cliché which is especially apropos for a situation like this: You win some, you lose so—"

"I don't lose any," Jason insisted. "I win them all!"

"Daddy!" Shannon shrieked as she saw her father coming toward them. She gave him a hero's welcome, fairly leaping from Sharla's arms into Case's, her baby face alight with joy.

Jason searched for the right words to console his friend on his humiliating strikeout. "Uh, tough luck, Case," he managed gruffly.

Case seemed more interested in his child's antics than in his softball performance. "Yeah, I guess it's about time those younger guys took over our title, huh, Fletch? We had a good run, though. Ten years, was it?"

"Eleven years," Jason corrected. His face was flushed. "And the title isn't lost yet, pal. We're going to win again this year and make it an even dozen." *Younger guys?* He cast a glance at twenty-six-year-old Zane Montrose, who was chatting up an admiring circle of nurses while the teams switched positions.

A dozen years ago, Jason Fletcher himself had been a first-year resident in orthopedics, a most promising one, who'd fulfilled that promise and gone on to become one of the Hospital Center's most skilled and successful orthopedic surgeons. He now had a flourishing practice, the awe and admiration of his patients, and the professional respect of his peers. He had achieved financial nirvana through talent, hard work, and excellent investments. And his popularity with women was the stuff of which hospital legends are made.

Jason's eyes narrowed as he watched the gaggle of pretty young women surrounding Montrose. When was the last time a whole group of young women had crowded around Jason Fletcher, their wide eyes hopeful and adoring? Not for a while, he realized, and then he realized something else. Something incredible, something unbelievable.

These days those nubile young women tended to address him as "sir," in the respectful tones reserved for their elders!

The revelation hit him with the driving force of a fastball.

"Jason, isn't your birthday on Monday?" Sharla's question was a welcome diversion. "Case and I are having our families over for a Labor Day cookout on Monday afternoon. Why don't you come?"

"We'll have a birthday cake for you," added Case, his eyes gleaming. "With forty candles blazing."

"I'm only going to be thirty-eight!" Jason protested hotly.

"That's close enough, old buddy," said Case, his expression suddenly turning serious. "Isn't it time to make some major changes in your life? Time to settle down and—"

"Help! Stop!" Jason held up his hand, as if to physically ward off the words. "No proselytizing allowed. Since you've been married, you're like a fanatical convert, Flynn. You want to bring everybody into the fold. But I have too much to do before I put on the old matrimonial ball and chain. There's too much fun to be had out there. I'm not ready to settle down to endless evenings of television with the little woman decked out in sweat socks and flannel bathrobe sitting beside me, complaining because I don't do the dishes often enough. As I've said so many times, marriage is an institution and I—"

"—don't want to live in an institution," Sharla finished for him. "Can't you update your material, Jason?"

Jason grinned. "For you, I'll work on it."

"Fletcher, come on, you're pitching!" shouted a teammate from the field.

"I'll let you know about Monday, Sharla." Jason grabbed Case's arm. "Come on, Flynn, we have a game to win."

Young Doctor Montrose wasn't the only one who'd pitched for his baseball team in college, Jason thought as he completed a satisfactory warm-up. Jason Fletcher had held the same position on *his* college team. And he could still throw a curve ball strong and fast enough to strike out the rangy pathologist who seldom struck out.

Zane Montrose was up next. Fletcher's team collectively groaned. "He'll hit another home run," lamented the shortstop, a portly obstetrician. "The kid is fantastic. Tell everybody in the outfield to move back about three miles."

Jason was irritated by the defeatist attitude; until this year, this game, defeat had been the opposing team's problem. Jason Fletcher's team had always felt confident because Jason Fletcher was on it. His presence assured victory.

Zane Montrose hit the ball so far that he reached the makeshift home plate long before Fletcher's hapless outfield managed to retrieve the ball. On the sidelines, a group of scrubbed-faced student nurses proclaimed "We're insane for Zane," while performing a rousing cheerleading routine.

"We just got here!" called the pretty, dark-haired, dark-eyed physical therapist as she hurried onto the field accompanied by another young woman. "Are we too late to play?"

Jason recognized the black-eyed beauty. She was Sharla's cousin, Dana Shakarian. Unlike her cousin, Dana had been known to catch the ball occasionally, although her hitting was as lamentable as Sharla's.

"Sure, you can play," Zane Montrose shouted eagerly. "Laura, want to be on our side?"

"No, Laura's going to be on our side," Jason interjected quickly. He didn't know Laura but he assumed she was the one standing quietly beside bouncy, lively Dana. The fact that Montrose had requested her presence sealed his determination to have her on his team.

"Well, since you guys are losing so badly, I guess it's only fair that you get first pick," Zane agreed, albeit with noticeable reluctance. "Come on, Dana. You're with us."

Jason's eyes flicked over his newest teammate. She was about five feet four and her oversized blue T-shirt and fashionably baggy blue-and-white striped shorts rendered androgynous whatever figure she might have. The slender delicacy of her arms and legs did not bode well for athletic strength though, he thought, glancing wistfully at the broad muscular build of the Shock/Trauma Unit's head nurse—who was on Montrose's team, of course. That woman was a powerhouse hitter.

Jason turned to his newest player, who was too small and too slightly built to be a powerhouse anything. Her face was almost completely shadowed by her cap, which was clearly too large for her. It covered all her hair as well. She looked like a lost waif, not the ballplayer needed to give the team a much needed boost.

"Pick up a glove and go to the farthest corner of the outfield," Jason said with a sigh. She'd do the team the least amount of damage way out there.

There were no left-handed gloves so Laura Novak fitted the standard model onto her left hand. She was accustomed to making do with right-handed equipment; left-handedness in a right-handed world required such adjustments. She tugged at the bill of her baseball cap as she trudged to the outer limits of the outfield. Everybody on both teams wore the caps provided by the picnic committee. Apparently this game was taken seriously by the participating personnel; Dana had warned her about that.

"But you *have* to come to the picnic!" Dana had insisted in that irrepressibly enthusiastic way of hers. "It's especially a must for a newcomer like you. You'll meet loads of people—everybody shows up for the annual picnic. And since you're the new head nurse on orthopedics, it's practically a command performance for you, if you know what I mean."

Laura knew exactly what she meant. Although she'd been in her new position at the Hospital Center for just two weeks, she knew enough hospital politics to know that staff members in positions of authority were required to attend certain functions that underlings could avoid with impunity. And while she was grateful that the outgoing, vivacious Dana had befriended her and insisted on driving her here, she felt strange and out of place and so very lonely, despite the crowds of people.

Laura took her position and tried to concentrate on the game. But there was nothing to do so far out in the outfield and her thoughts kept intruding. Today was the third anniversary of the worst day of her life and she'd rather have endured it at home with her family than with this rollicking group of strangers.

She glanced down at the small diamond ring which she wore on the third finger of her right hand. It had been her engagement ring; now it was a cherished memento of a long-ago dream. She'd switched it from her left hand to her right on the day of her fiancé's funeral. Three years ago.

Laura's eyes flicked to her watch and she noted the time: four-fifteen. This time three years ago, she had been preparing for her wedding, which was to be held at five o'clock in the small-town church she'd worshipped in since childhood. This time three years ago her beloved Danny was still alive, clowning with his brother Tom as they donned what they called their "monkey suits" for the wedding.

Except the wedding had never taken place. A drunk in a pickup truck smashed head-on into Danny's car as he and Tom were driving to the church.

It had been a big news story in the Washington-Baltimore area for several days. Local TV stations had broadcast film clips, telling the tragic tale of the young bridegroom's death just a few blocks from the church where his bride awaited him. His older brother and best man was critically injured. The tragedy had plunged the small suburban town of Farview, Maryland, into stunned mourning.

Shouts and shrieks jarred Laura from her melancholy reverie. The softball was flying into the outfield and her teammates were doing a spectacular job of missing it. Swiftly, she ran forward, her arm extended, and caught the ball in her glove. She threw it immediately to the pitcher and he tagged the runner, caught between third base and home plate.

A potential home run had been converted into an out! Jason was ecstatic. That new girl—what was her name?—actually knew what she was doing! Unlike the other assorted turkeys on this hapless team, she'd gone after the ball, instead of staring at it as it whizzed by. And she'd caught it! She'd also known to throw it to him, instead of standing there, looking dumbfounded, which the other players in the outfield tended to do.

"I want her in the infield," Jason shouted and promptly sent one of the dopes who'd blithely watched the ball sail by to change places with Laura in the outer outfield.

"Nice play," he said as she took her new position.

"Thanks." Laura smiled. The pitcher certainly was intensely involved in the game. And his attitude was contagious. She pushed her traumatic memories to the back of her mind and concentrated fully on softball. She made another catch and threw it to the first baseman, a left-handed radiologist, preventing the runner from going on to second base. Then she caught a pop fly, giving the team its third out.

"Can you hit as well as you field?" Jason asked her hopefully as the team walked off the field to take their turn at bat.

"I played on my high school and nursing school softball teams and I used to be able to get a hit every time I was up at bat," Laura told him. "But I haven't played since graduation."

"You're new at the Hospital Center," Jason concluded, "or you'd have been playing at the picnic every year." And he would have remembered her. He made it a point to know who was a good player and who wasn't.

She nodded. "I started two weeks ago in—"

"Laura, are you up this inning?" Zane Montrose called from the pitcher's mound. "Let's try a couple of practice hits."

Laura groaned. "Why doesn't he offer someone else a chance to practice hit?" she murmured, deliberately not glancing in his direction.

"Laura, hey, Laura," persisted Zane, "grab a bat and let's hit a few."

Jason glanced at her, his expression thoughtful. "Can it be that our boy Zane has a crush on you?"

She winced. "I—I wish he'd just leave me alone." Players on both teams were looking from her to Zane, and she didn't welcome the attention. Her brief, involuntary stint in the ghoulish media glare following Danny's death had made her acutely sensitive to the stares and whispers of others.

"Take him up on his offer," Jason recommended. "If you haven't played for awhile, it'll be a good opportunity to brush up on your hitting."

"But I don't want to encourage him to—"

"It's for the team." Jason's gray eyes gleamed. "I'll protect you from zany Zane's pitches off the field, I promise."

Reluctantly, Laura picked up a bat. Jason watched her swing at Zane's practice throws. He noticed that Montrose pitched differently to Laura than to the other players. He threw the ball right to her; there were no tricky curves or intimidating speed. He wanted her to hit the ball.

And when Laura hit a triple, Zane cheered as lustily as her own teammates. When Jason hit her home—and got himself to second base—Montrose shouted out his congratulations to Laura for making a run.

"Whose team is that clown rooting for, anyway?" Jason complained to Case. "His own or Laura's?"

"You've been out of the country," Case said with a chuckle. "So you don't know about Zane Montrose's pursuit of the elusive Laura. I, on the other hand, know more about it than I ever wanted to know, because Sharla's cousin Dana has the hots for Zane."

Jason frowned. Hospital gossip usually amused him; he'd certainly been the focus of it himself often enough. But for reasons he couldn't begin to fathom, he found nothing amusing about this latest potential triangle.

The game continued. By the end of the last inning, Jason was forced to face the unthinkable. Despite his most valiant efforts and some excellent plays by various other members of his team, the fact—and the score—were irrefutable. Jason Fletcher's team was going to lose the game. For the first time in twelve years, he wasn't the winning pitcher on the winning team.

It didn't help that everyone kept slapping him on the back and making jovially inane remarks like "The king is dead, long live the king." Or "It's the end of an era." And the ever-atrocious "You win some, you lose some."

Jason played the required role of good sport. He flashed a hearty grin. He managed to choke out, "It doesn't matter if you win or lose, it's how you play the game," although he didn't believe it for a minute. He even shook Zane Montrose's hand and praised his pitching skills.

But depression descended over him like a shroud. It really was the end of an era. The winning streak was broken. He was pushing forty and a younger man had taken over. In softball. In hospital gossip. The fatiguing jet lag he'd managed to keep at bay during the game hit him with full force. He was exhausted; he had to get home and get some sleep. Though the picnic traditionally lasted late into the night, Jason decided to leave immediately. Another first. In the past, he was always one of the last to leave the picnic; now he was leaving earlier than the families with little kids.

"The food's almost ready. Will you sit with me at dinner, Laura?" Zane Montrose's voice filtered through Jason's cloud of gloom. He turned to see Zane and Laura standing a few feet behind him.

A definitely perverse streak prompted Jason to reply, "Sorry, kid, she promised to eat with me."

"Yes, I did promise to eat with him, Zane," Laura said quickly. She hurried to catch up to Jason, leaving the younger man without a backward glance.

"Thanks," she said softly as she trotted beside him toward the main pavilion where the food was being served.

"The pleasure is all mine. Montrose might've scored big every time he got up to bat, but he sure struck out with you!" The notion warmed him.

"We haven't actually been introduced," he said, turning to her with a smile. He was positively delighted with this unexpected turn of events. Zane Montrose was staring after them, his shoulders slumped, his expression glum. "I'm Jason Fletcher."

"I figured that out from all the yelling and cheering during the game," Laura said. "You're the orthopedic surgeon who's been away for the past month, aren't you? I'm—"

"I've been away six weeks," he interrupted, correcting her. He wasn't surprised that she'd heard of him; he would have been amazed, not to mention slightly piqued, if she hadn't. His smile broadened. "And I know you're Laura from the yells and cheers, and that you're a nurse because you were on your nursing school softball team. But I didn't catch your last name."

"Novak. Laura Novak. And I'm—"

"Well, I'm pleased to meet you, Laura Novak." He interrupted her once again.

A smile played around the corners of Laura's mouth. It looked as if she was never going to get the chance to tell him that she was the new head nurse on the orthopedics floor, and that as a result they would be working together daily.

"You're one helluva softball player," Jason continued lightly. "And now would you mind taking off your cap so I can see what you look like?"

Her cheeks flushing, Laura pulled off her cap. A mop of thick, light brown hair, blunt cut, tumbled nearly to her shoulders. She had a beautifully smooth peaches-and-cream complexion and wide-set eyes that were an unusual light mixture of blue, green, and gray. Her features were delicate—a small, straight nose, a firm little chin, and a well-shaped mouth with even white teeth.

She was cute. And she was with him. Jason smiled with satisfaction. Young Montrose might have won the game, but Jason Fletcher had walked off with the girl. His mood lightened considerably.

The situation reminded him of an article he'd read in a *National Geographic* at the dentist's office. Something about a young buck challenging and locking antlers with the established leader of the forest. Or had they been male chimps in the jungle?

He gave an impatient shrug. Whatever. In the animal kingdom, the winner of the confrontation was the one who got the female. And in today's version of the primal contest, that would be himself. Jason Fletcher.

Two

A buffet featuring fried chicken, hamburgers, hot dogs, potato salad, cole slaw, fruit salad, tossed green salad, and pasta salad covered two tables in the pavilion. A third table boasted a tempting assortment of desserts: candy, cupcakes, cookies, and brownies.

Jason filled his plate. "I'm starving. I haven't had anything to eat since I left Belfast. The food on the plane was abominable."

"Belfast?" Laura stared at him. "Do you mean Northern Ireland?"

Jason chuckled. "I wasn't vacationing there, I was working. I spent the last six weeks at the Royal Victoria Hospital observing their treatment of gunshot wounds. Their vascular and orthopedic expertise in that area is recognized around the world. They have yet to lose a limb from low-velocity gunshot injuries."

Laura was impressed. "In the two weeks since I've been at the Hospital Center, there's been a teenage boy who lost his leg in a gunfight with a policeman."

Jason grimaced. "We've had too many cases like that. When I read about the program in Belfast, I couldn't wait to get over there. Here in Washington, we see more gunshot wounds to bones in one week than they do in a month over there. The statistics seem skewed because their violence is political and more public."

She followed him to a table in a nearby pavilion and listened while he described the techniques he'd learned for repairing a kneecap shattered by a bullet. "The way they do it, the patient ends up walking with a limp. Using our current techniques, the patient might not ever walk at all."

He laid down his plastic fork and frowned. "Montrose is heading this way. Odds are, he'll attempt to join us."

"Oh no!" Laura's expression was a mixture of dismay and disgust.

Jason suppressed a pleased smile. "You're really not interested in him? You're not just playing hard to get?"

Shaking her head, she leaned forward, her blue-green-gray eyes large. "He made a pass at me the first day he met me," she whispered, clearly distressed by the memory. "He grabbed me right in the corridor on my way to the cafeteria for lunch."

"What nerve!" Jason strove to appear shocked and outraged. He felt a lot like a wolf donning the disguise of a sheep.

"The director of nursing's office was just two doors away." Laura shuddered. "Suppose she'd have come out and found me there in a clinch with him? She wouldn't have known that *he'd* grabbed *me*. You can imagine what an incident like that would do to my reputation!"

"Scandalous," agreed Jason. "Montrose is an animal." And a world-class jerk, he added smugly to himself. The first rule in making a successful pass was to be sure the lady was willing. And anyone but a half-wit could guess that a newly hired nurse would hardly be willing to engage in a hot clinch with the director of nursing, the boss of bosses, nearby.

"He's always hanging around me. I've never been in this situation before," Laura confided anxiously. "My relationships with the doctors at Farview, the hospital where I worked before, were completely professional." She didn't bother to add that there wasn't a doctor under the age of fifty-five practicing at Farview Memorial. It was the principle that mattered. "I want it to be the same way here."

Jason stifled a grin. Little Laura had a lot to learn about relationships in a big city hospital. There were plenty of them that went far beyond the professional. And nobody cared, as long as it didn't interfere with patient care.

"Hey, is there room for me here?" Zane Montrose joined them, his voice hearty and hopeful.

"Sure." Jason stood up. "Laura and I were just leaving." He glanced across the pavilion to see Dana Shakarian about to sit down at a table. Dana was a good kid, and she deserved a break, he decided. "Dana," he called. "There's room over here."

Dana arrived at the table a few seconds later. "Sit down here, next to Montrose," suggested Jason. He felt rather avuncular playing Cupid. "Laura and I are on our way out of here."

"You're leaving now?" asked Dana as she slipped onto the bench beside Zane, her dark eyes glowing with anticipation. "Is Jason taking you home, Laura?"

Jason watched Zane open his mouth to offer a ride and took great pleasure in saying firmly, "Yes, I'm taking Laura home. Whenever she's ready to leave."

"I'd like to go now," Laura said quickly. She'd fulfilled her duty, she assured herself. She'd participated, she'd been seen at the annual picnic. The prospect of going home held infinite appeal.

It did to Jason too. How many hours had it been since he'd last slept? He couldn't remember, but the exhaustion he kept managing to postpone struck him again. "Let's go," he said, cupping Laura's elbow with his hand to lead her away.

"You'll be Dana's friend forever," Laura murmured. "She's crazy about Zane Montrose. That's another reason why I don't want him pestering me. Dana's been so nice and friendly to me since I came to the Hospital Center."

"And you don't want Montrose to ruin your budding friendship with Dana," concluded Jason. He cast a quick glance back at the table to see an animated Dana conversing with Zane, who was still looking rather disconsolate. Jason grinned.

Laura was aware of the interested, speculative glances cast their way as they left the pavilion. It took them a long time to leave. Jason stopped at almost every table to engage in a few moments of small talk, and he introduced Laura each time, his fingers on her elbow lightly but purposefully keeping her by his side.

She watched him during the brief, amiable conversations and found herself admiring his easy ability to talk to everyone, from the maintenance crew to the lordly attending physicians. She liked the smooth, self-confident way he carried himself, the rangy elegant movements of his big, muscular frame. He was the type of man who commanded notice however large the crowd.

She noticed other women watching him, felt their glances flicker over her too. Oddly, the attention didn't bother her. She wondered why. A short while ago, she'd been cringing at the visibility Zane Montrose's unwelcome attentions had brought her. But being seen at Jason Fletcher's side had an entirely different effect upon her. It seemed natural to be there; she felt proud to be with him.

"I think I've met more people during this walk through the pavilions than I met during the entire span of my career at Farview Memorial," she remarked lightly as they finally left the picnickers and headed toward the parking lot. "You know everybody and they all know you." Quiet and reserved by nature, she admired his natural gregariousness.

"Yeah, Mr. Popularity." Jason flashed a disarming, self-mocking grin. "That's me."

Laura's eyes kept straying to the man at her side. His compelling masculinity seemed impossible to ignore. At six three, he possessed the powerful build of a lifelong athlete. His skill and strength during the game attested to the fact. And though they'd played nine innings of softball, his well-fitting khaki slacks and wine-colored polo shirt still somehow appeared crisp and unrumpled.

He was the kind of man she would normally back away from, for the intense virility and electric sexuality he effortlessly projected were too powerful for inhibited, controlled Laura. But their combined efforts during the softball game had let her see another side of him, devoid of the threatening, powerful sexuality. She enjoyed athletic competition and recognized a fellow sportsman in Jason.

And unlike Zane Montrose, who embarrassed her with his blatant and unwanted pursuit, Jason Fletcher's behavior toward her had been reassuringly casual and friendly.

They stopped at a sleek black two-door hardtop which bore the legend Jaguar XJS next to the taillights. "Like it?" Jason asked proudly, and she knew she was supposed to swoon over the car. Her sister Lianna would have, she thought, and her mouth curved into a wry smile. Lianna had a thing for expensive, fast sports cars; she would consider the exotic car wasted on sensible, prosaic Laura.

"It's a nice car," Laura said politely.

"Honey, visiting a senior citizen is nice. Taking a dog for a walk in the park is nice. This car is way beyond mere *nice*."

Laura smiled demurely, her light eyes teasing, "*Very* nice, then?"

Jason's comically exaggerated expression of exasperation made her laugh. The sound of her laughter drew his attention to her, and he stared at her, suddenly seeing her in a whole new way. Her face was alight, her eyes bright and sparkling. His heart thumped oddly. At this moment, her looks far exceeded "cute." Even "pretty" was too lame a word to describe the glowing and animated young woman standing before him.

He couldn't seem to drag his gaze away from her. Standing there, her face alive with laughter, her hair rustled by the warm September breeze, he thought she was the loveliest thing he'd ever seen.

The force and depth of his gaze drew her eyes to him, and her breath caught tightly in her throat. His gray eyes were warm and aware, and the curve of his well-shaped mouth held explosive sensual promise. A slow spiral of heat began to uncoil deep within her, and she felt her cheeks flush. Her pulses began to race, and she didn't know whether it was from fear or anticipation or a curious mixture of them both.

Shaken, she took a small step back. The unexpected, swift spark of desire unnerved her. Never before had she simply looked into a man's eyes and felt the exciting stirring of arousal. She had always been controlled, reserved, inhibited, always governed by her head and never by her hormones. Not even with Danny had she . . .

The thought of her poor lost Danny catapulted her into a spasm of guilt. If Danny had lived, they would be celebrating their third wedding anniversary today—they might have even had a child by now. But Danny was in his grave and here she stood, gazing at another man and feeling so very much alive. She couldn't control the quickening of her blood or the syrupy heat coursing through her. It was as if she were coming fully awake after a long, numbing trance.

Jason was the first to drop his gaze. He saw the sudden flare of sexual awareness in her eyes and read it for what it was. So often in the past when he had seen that particular look in a woman's eyes, he'd acted upon it like the smooth operator he considered himself to be.

So why wasn't he making a move on Laura? he asked himself as he inserted the car key into the lock. He'd seen the way she looked at him. He was an experienced man, he knew he could make her want him before she was even aware that she was being seduced. Yet he knew he wasn't going to act on his impulses.

Because she was young and sweet and sincere, not his type at all, he reminded himself. He disregarded age only if a woman possessed a discernible sexual sangfroid, which made her fair game according to his own certain code of ethics. He was something of an expert in sorting out those women who could or could not handle the kind of casual, uncomplicated relationship he preferred. He'd been wrong a few times, and quickly broke things off when he realized the woman didn't know the rules of the game—or chose to ignore them.

He believed in good sportsmanship and that extended to all areas of his life. It wouldn't be sporting to lure earnest, wide-eyed Laura into his bed, not when he instinctively, subconsciously knew that a relationship between the two of them would be anything but casual and uncomplicated. And the stubbornly carefree bachelor in him backed away at the prospect of intensity and complexity.

Jason climbed into the car and leaned across both seats to swing open the door to the passenger side. "Get in," he ordered, trying to mask the huskiness of his voice. His body was tightening and a pleasant heaviness suffused his loins. Muttering an expletive, he tried to will away the physical effect she was having on him.

Laura got into the car and pulled the door closed. There was a palpable sexual tension between them, which she somehow found both threatening and exciting. She glanced covertly at his striking profile, at his thick, dark brown hair which looked intriguingly tempting to touch. Laura gulped. Shocked by her uncharacteristic impulse, she kept her hands folded firmly in her lap.

Jason made no attempt to start the car. "How old are you?" he asked bluntly, studying her.

She stared at him in surprise. "Twenty-four." Her beautiful eyes were quizzical. "I'll be twenty-five on New Year's Eve. Uh, why?"

Jason shrugged. "Just wondering. You don't look almost twenty-five," he added a bit gruffly. "You look about the same age as those ditzy student nurses who were all but drooling over Montrose."

"I'm not sure how to take that," Laura said, her eyes lighting with quiet humor. "Was that a compliment or an insult?"

Jason chuckled. "Both, I think. I'd find it easier to ignore you if you were a silly teenager. But you're a mature woman—not that it changes anything."

She stared at him, confused.

"You're not even sure what I'm talking about, are you?" Jason asked dryly. "You've just reaffirmed my decision. I'm taking you directly home. Which is?" He glanced at her expectantly.

"This conversation is like trying to type on a typewriter with the key letters missing," Laura said wryly. Vital connections kept being missed, making logical transition impossible.

"Where do you live, Laura?" Jason asked with exaggerated patience. Did she have any idea how appealing she looked as she puzzled over the quick throwaway lines he passed off as conversation?

he wondered. She was so serious, so cute. He reminded himself again that serious and cute, sweet and sincere, inevitably led to expectations that he didn't care to fulfill.

Laura shifted in her seat, feeling uncomfortable under his watchful gray gaze. From the hot looks they'd exchanged outside the car, she was certain that he was as attracted to her as she was to him. Every feminine instinct she possessed told her that he wanted her, yet he hadn't made a grab for her the way Zane Montrose had when he'd looked at her with masculine hunger in his eyes.

The sinking feeling of disappointment she felt at the realization that Jason Fletcher wasn't even going to try to touch her astonished her.

"Those big eyes of yours are very expressive, Laura," Jason said with a slight laugh. "You're worried that I'm about to pounce on you, like our boy Zane."

She swallowed. He'd scrambled the message which he claimed to have read in her "big expressive eyes." "I know you're not," she said rather breathlessly. What if he were to pounce? What if he were to lean across the seat to pull her against the solid strength of his chest, to hold her there with his strong, muscular arms? A sensual little shiver tingled along her spine.

"If I did, at least you wouldn't have to worry about the director of nursing catching you," Jason said with a smile so charming that the air seemed to whoosh from her lungs in a gasp. "We know she's safely occupied back at the grill, stuffing hot dogs into rolls."

Laura gave a nervous little nod and tried to toss off an insouciant smile. The image of herself in a passionate embrace with Jason was doing wild things to her heart rate. She had a strong feeling that if she were in Jason's arms, the whereabouts of the director of nursing would be utterly irrelevant to her.

The thought of himself and Laura in a hot clinch was affecting Jason too. He busied himself with starting the car, and the engine raced to life. "Fasten your seatbelt," he ordered as he buckled his own. "When you've seen as much damage done to passengers in car accidents as I have, you don't drive two feet without everyone in the car strapped in."

His voice brooked no argument and Laura buckled up. She knew the statistics as well as anybody. Seatbelts saved lives in ninety per cent of all accidents. That left ten percent where they didn't matter at all. Danny's accident had been one in that hopeless ten percent; the seatbelt he'd been wearing hadn't saved him.

Jason cleared his throat. "You still haven't told me where you want to go."

Laura forced herself to shake off her dark thoughts. "I live in Farview with my aunt and uncle," she said. "It's—"

"—one of those little towns north of Baltimore?" Jason cut in. "Along I-ninety-five?" Laura nodded, and he suppressed a groan. "That's a good forty-five minutes from here," he said, half wishing Zane Montrose was the one making the trip, after all. He was exhausted and now he had a ninety-minute drive facing him before he could fall into bed. "Why do you live so far from the hospital? Isn't the commute a killer?"

"I just started at the Hospital Center two weeks ago," Laura said softly. "So far the drive hasn't been too bad."

"It adds ninety minutes to your workday," Jason said dampeningly as he pulled out of the parking lot and followed the winding two-lane road out of the park. "Why don't you get a place in DC or one of the suburban apartment complexes closer to the hospital?" He sure wished she were living in such a place now.

"I probably will," she said noncommittally and

then added, "I'm sorry to take you so far out of your way, especially after your flight and all. You must be exhausted. Why don't you take me back to the picnic and I'll ask Dana to give me a ride home?" Her voice was warm and concerned, and she'd stated exactly what he longed to do.

But having been offered the option, Jason now found it unthinkable. "I'm not *that* tired. I said I'd take you home and I will." He shot her a sudden, amused grin. "Anyway, you wouldn't want to put a crimp in Dana's conquest of Zane, would you?"

"No!" Laura shook her head so vigorously that they both laughed.

"I keep meaning to ask you," Jason said, still smiling. "Where do you work in the hospital? In what department?" They were just a short distance from the intersection where the park road fed into a major divided highway.

Laura never had a chance to answer his question, for seemingly out of nowhere, a blue pickup truck roared into their line of vision. The truck was traveling at high speed as it approached them, and veered alarmingly toward the middle of the road.

"Drunken fool," Jason muttered harshly and slowed the Jaguar considerably. "I've spent too many hours in surgery trying to put back together what menaces like him have—"

He never completed the sentence. For the blue pickup truck had crossed the lane and was heading directly toward them. And while the Jaguar had slowed to a virtual crawl, the truck's speed was increasing. And continuing to build.

It happened so fast. Paradoxically, those few seconds seemed to freeze into some timeless frame enabling Laura to experience the entire episode in a kind of bizarre slow-motion sequence.

She saw the pickup truck speeding toward them and knew that a head-on crash was inevitable.

The Jaguar was small; it would offer no protection from the force of such a collision. A pickup truck. Three years ago today, there had been another accident involving a pickup truck. A fatal accident.

Laura's mind seemed to detach itself; sheer terror set it spinning. Suddenly it was as if she were in that car with Danny and Tom three years ago on the way to the church when that other pickup truck had smashed into them. So this was the way Danny had felt, seeing the truck coming at his car, knowing it was going to hit. So numbed by shock and fear that it seemed unreal, yet knowing rationally that this was the end. The end . . . Laura shut her eyes tightly and tried to pray.

A scream seemed to echo in her head. The car jerked and bumped and finally came to an abrupt halt. Laura couldn't breathe, couldn't move. She was trapped in a black void, rendered helpless by icy panic and overwhelming despair.

For a few moments she felt suspended between two worlds. In one, there was an eerie silence, in another her ears rang with screams. Slowly, gradually, other sounds filtered into her consciousness. The sound of a car door slamming. The sound of a man's voice swearing. Using some words that she'd never heard before, and others that would've earned her a mouthful of soapsuds back in her childhood, had she dared to use them.

Laura opened her eyes. The black void disappeared. She was strapped in her seat in the Jaguar which was resting in a ditch, half covered by a spate of overgrown branches. As if in a dream, she slowly turned her head to see the driver's seat empty and the door standing wide open.

Moments later, Jason leaned inside. "That maniac could've killed us!" His voice was hard and brusque and furious. "Did you happen to see his license plate? I tried to get the numbers but he was going too damn fast. He's already out of sight.

I'm going to report him to the police. Maybe they'll nail him before he does kill someone."

Adrenaline poured through his veins like liquid fire. The horrible fear he'd felt upon seeing the truck heading right for them had been transposed into a fiery rage. He punched the buttons of his car phone to report the incident.

Laura sat trembling in her seat and listened to him relate the details of the near miss. She couldn't seem to stop shaking; she felt freezing cold and sick to her stomach, too, as if she'd suddenly been stricken with a violent flu bug. She closed her eyes and leaned her head back against the headrest, trying to swallow the nausea produced by her churning stomach.

But the moment she closed her eyes, she saw the blue pickup truck coming toward them. And she heard screams, and there was pain and blood and death. . . .

Laura jerked her eyes open and covered her face with her hands, desperately trying to block out the sight and the sounds. She breathed deeply, and very slowly the horror began to recede. Jason's voice, raised and angry, penetrated the fog enshrouding her mind.

"No, no one was hurt. No, there was no actual collision," he shouted into the receiver of his car phone at whomever was on the other end of the line. "I already told you, I managed to swerve into a ditch at the very last second to avoid being hit. But there's a drunken psychopath out on the road who needs to be stopped before he sends a carload of innocent people to the morgue."

Laura flinched. She closed her eyes and saw the truck barreling toward them again, its headlights and grillwork suddenly converted into a grotesquely demonic grill. Her eyes flew open.

"*There's nothing you can do without the license plate number?*" Jason snarled into the phone. "*I should've made a note of it?* Hey, mister, *you* try reading a license plate coming toward you at ninety-plus miles an hour while you're trying to get the hell out of its path! Dammit, I'm not swearing! What do you mean, there's no need to become verbally abusive? We were almost killed, you moron! And now—Hello? Hello?"

"Damn!" He turned to Laura, outraged. "They hung up on me. Gave me a lecture about license plates and telephone manners and then hung up!"

It took a moment for the red haze of fury to lift, but when it did, Jason's eyes widened in concern at the sight of her. "Laura, are you all right? You're whiter than a ghost. Are you hurt?"

Her ashen face and dilated pupils alarmed him. He told himself that she couldn't be hurt, that there had been no collision, that she'd been safely belted into her seat and the impact of the car into the ditch had been minimal. But even as he attempted to reassure himself, he reached for her pulse. It was weak and thready, and he carefully moved his hands over her, touching, probing, seeking. Could she somehow have sustained internal injuries, he wondered. It seemed impossible, but he examined her belly thoroughly, feeling for the telltale rigidity which signified internal bleeding.

There was none. Having ruled out physical injury, his second diagnosis was hysteria. Another careful scrutiny of her cloudy eyes and benumbed expression confirmed it. He took both her hands in his and spoke, very slowly and firmly. "Laura, it's all right. It was a close call, but nothing happened. We're okay."

She shivered. His words tumbled around in her head. She felt cold and alone, and when she tried to smile and speak, she couldn't. Her mouth felt too dry to form the words and her lips twisted into a quivering grimace. Tears filled her eyes and slid down her cheeks and she could do nothing to stop the involuntary flow.

"Don't cry!" Jason stared at her. "Laura, everything is all right."

He felt shaken and out of his depth. As a doctor who spent his life caring for patients in pain, many of them with critical injuries, he had learned long ago to distance himself from their emotional reactions. He had to; he couldn't function medically if he were to become overinvolved emotionally.

But the ability to distance and detach himself had crept into other areas of his life, as he well knew. With women, for instance. He expected his female companions to be bright and breezy, to keep things light and fun. He had no time or interest in a deeper relationship with the accompanying deeper emotions, and over the years he'd found it easier and easier to withdraw from a woman's tears and needs. He could cope with a crying woman if she were his patient, but not if she were a date.

"I—I feel so stupid," Laura managed to say. "I know we're okay. It's just the—the date. My fiancé was killed in a car accident three years ago today. And when I saw that truck . . . I—I saw the crash again. I heard it!"

Jason's apprehensions vanished. This was hardly a social situation, and his natural compassion overrode his clinical detachment. "You poor little girl, no wonder you're so upset. It must've seemed like a horrifying case of déjà vu, seeing that truck coming at us."

He leaned across the console and put one arm around her; reaching into the tiny backseat for the box of tissues with his other. He plunked the box into her lap, then plucked a tissue out and put it into her hand.

"It was so dark," Laura whispered, her eyes fixed ahead. "I heard the screams and then it was so quiet. So deathly still."

Jason guessed that she was reliving the tragic, fatal accident and instinctively drew her closer.

"Was your fiancé driving?" he asked quietly. "Or were you?"

"I wasn't in the car." Laura gulped back a sob. She couldn't stop crying; the harder she tried, the harder she cried. It was disconcerting and embarrassing, and more than a little scary, too. Laura was accustomed to being in complete control of herself; she never let her emotions take over. But this time her emotions had burst through, overthrowing her tight control the way zealous revolutionaries topple a totalitarian government.

"You weren't in the car? But I thought you said you saw the other car coming toward you and you heard the crash?"

Yes, she had. Laura began to tremble violently. When she'd seen that pickup truck about to hit them, she'd somehow experienced the horror of the accident firsthand, as if she'd been there. "M-Maybe it was some psychic transference, some kind of ESP," she whispered.

Jason coughed discreetly. "Honey, I sincerely doubt it. As a practitioner in the science of medicine, I'm grounded in reality and highly skeptical of psychic phenomena. And that's putting it mildly."

"It must have been, Jason." Laura sat up, frantically trying to wipe away her tears with the now sodden tissue. "It was as if I were really there, in the car."

Jason handed her another tissue and said nothing.

"You don't believe me." For some reason, that made Laura cry harder.

"Baby, you're overwrought." Jason pulled her back to him. Her head rested against his chest and he stroked her silky hair with his big, rough palm. "You're not thinking clearly. Now I want you to relax. Breathe deeply. Close your eyes and let yourself—"

"It was on our wedding day," Laura said softly. She spoke as if dazed. "Three years ago today. It was a few minutes before five o'clock and I was in the church and the organ was playing when the police came to tell me about Danny's accident. He was just five blocks away. I wanted to go there immediately, but my uncle George wouldn't let me."

Jason drew in a sharp breath. "My God, I remember that accident—the young bridegroom who was killed just a few minutes before his wedding. It was front-page news in both the Washington and Baltimore papers. There was a survivor who was brought to the Hospital Center's Shock/ Trauma Unit by the Life Flight Helicopter."

Laura nodded. "That was Tom, Danny's brother. He was going to be the best man at our wedding. He had massive internal injuries and Dr. Flynn operated on him and saved his life."

"You were the bride." Jason stared down at her, concern and compassion etched in his face. "I'm so sorry, Laura. Everyone in the Shock/Trauma Unit was affected by that accident. We see a lot of tragedy, but that one was exceptionally grim." His arms tightened protectively around her. "We sometimes wondered what happened to that young bride. I guess we all hoped that she'd met some nice guy and married him."

"Oh no, I couldn't have married someone else." The very thought distressed her. "For a long time, I couldn't bear to think of even dating another man." She swallowed. "I still haven't dated. Until I came to the Hospital Center, I worked the night shift at Farview Memorial and slept during the days. Sometimes I worked a double shift. That kind of schedule pretty much precludes a social life, even if I'd wanted one."

Jason frowned. Three years without a date? Did that mean what he thought it meant: three years without sex? He couldn't fathom it. "Er, don't you ever—uh—get lonely?" He tried to phrase it tactfully.

Laura shook her head, oblivious to his innuendo. "I live with my aunt Sally and uncle George and they're positively wonderful." The thought of her relatives and their loving patience and kindness made emotional tears begin to flow again. "S-Sometimes my sister lives with us too. She moves in and out, depending on what's going on in her life—which is usually a mess," she added, gulping back a sob.

Her head lay against the solid warmth of Jason's chest and she could hear the reassuring beat of his heart beneath her ear. She took a deep breath and inhaled the musky masculine scent of him, a heady aroma of perspiration and soap and man. Danny's accident and their sadly aborted wedding seemed far, far away. Three long years away from the present where, in Jason's arms, she felt safe from fear and pain and grief.

Her hands had been clenched in her lap, but slowly, as if of their own volition, they moved toward Jason's inviting warmth. The fabric of his cotton shirt felt soft and the muscular strength beneath it radiated a virile heat. Her lids fluttered closed.

And suddenly she was in the backseat of a car, hearing screams, feeling a terror she didn't understand. She saw the headlights coming toward her, growing closer and larger, blinding her. There was a deafening, jolting crash and she felt herself slam into something hard. When she looked around again, there was darkness and a silence more frightening than anything she had ever known.

Laura bolted upright with a heart-stopping scream.

Three

"Laura, it's all right." Jason's voice, soothing yet firm, sounded above her. He was holding her again, smoothing her hair and her back in long, slow sweeps with his big, capable hands.

She felt so soft and delicate in his arms. His lips brushed the top of her hair which smelled of a pleasing-scented herbal shampoo. This was new to him, simply holding a woman to offer her comfort. Normally when Jason Fletcher took a woman in his arms, it was as a prelude to sex.

Laura shuddered and snuggled closer. Jason decided that he liked comforting her. Very much. "It's all over, honey. All over. You're safe now with me."

His voice poured over her like warm honey. Laura clung to him, savoring the security of his masculine strength. It seemed natural to confide in him. "Every time I close my eyes I'm there. It's—It's like some kind of weird flashback," she whispered. "But it can't be a flashback because I wasn't there." She told him about her vision of being in the backseat and seeing the headlights, about hearing the screams and the deathly silence.

Jason listened carefully. What she was describing seemed like a hallucination to him. He'd worked extensively with accident survivors and knew such tricks of the mind were possible, even common. He supposed that the emotional trauma of losing a loved one in an accident could produce similar symptoms, even in those survivors who hadn't been in the accident.

One thing was certain. He couldn't drive forty-five minutes to Farview with her in this state. "Laura, I'm going to take you to my place. It's about ten minutes from here and—"

"No, please, I just want to go home!"

The note of panic in her voice convinced him that he was right not to risk the drive just yet. When she began to struggle, he tightened his grip on her, anchoring her firmly against him. "I'll take you home later. But right now you need a little time to pull yourself together. I don't want you going into hysterics while—"

"I won't go into hysterics! I've never been hysterical in my entire life!"

"Laura, I'm trained to make a diagnosis based on the presenting symptoms. And the symptoms you're presenting right now are those of hysteria induced by an emotional shock."

She felt like screaming again, and almost did. Her emotional volatility stunned her, dismayed her too. She prided herself on her strength, on her staunch self-control. At Danny's funeral, she'd been the only one who hadn't cried. She'd been a bulwark of strength for his family and her own.

Inhaling deeply, she pulled herself away from Jason's arms and sat up straight. "I'm fine now," she said in a shaky voice she hardly recognized as her own. She fumbled with the buckle of her seatbelt, trying to reclasp it, but her hands were trembling so much she couldn't manage it.

"Sure. You're doing just great," Jason said dryly, watching her struggle with the clasp. He reached over and fastened it for her. "Now try closing your eyes for a second."

"No!" she exclaimed too quickly in a voice that was too shrill.

"You're afraid to do it."

"Of course I'm not. Afraid to close my eyes? Don't be ridiculous!" Her voice was rising again, and to her horror, she started to cry once more.

Jason stared at her for a moment and then started the car. Laura tried to stem the tide of tears that seemed to flow nonstop. A futile endeavor. Her lack of control appalled her. She was aware of Jason casting quick, concerned glances at her from the corner of his eye as he steered the Jaguar through the Saturday evening traffic.

She couldn't bear to think what he must think of her! How were they going to be able to work together after this episode? she wondered in despair. How could he take her seriously in her position as head nurse on his floor when he'd seen her behaving like an out-of-control crybaby? And how could she face him without cringing in memory of her own breakdown?

Such tormenting thoughts were hardly bolstering. Instead of sternly snapping herself out of her mortifying condition as she'd intended, Laura exacerbated it.

They arrived at his condominium, a complex of luxury townhouses sporting an Olympic-size pool, tennis and racquetball courts, and a putting green, which Jason pointed out to Laura in a conversational attempt to divert her.

It didn't work. Deep, involuntary sobs continued to convulse her. Frowning with concern, Jason pulled his car into the small carport adjacent to his condo and stared at her. "Can you walk or do you want me to carry you?"

Laura gazed around her. A peculiar lassitude engulfed her. "I—I want to go home."

"I'll take you home as soon as I'm sure you

won't flip out on the freeway. I can't drive and look after you at the same time. I'm not about to risk another accident." He climbed out of the car and came around to her side to open the door, extending a hand to assist her from the car.

Flip out on the freeway! Laura flushed scarlet. Her worst fear had been confirmed. He thought she was a freaked-out hysteric—and no wonder! Humiliation washed over her in waves, heightening the terrible confusion that gripped her. "I—I don't know what's the matter with me," she whispered.

She looked so small and scared. Something indefinable about her appealed to him, drawing him to her in a way he could neither explain nor understand. Jason Fletcher was a cheerfully confident extrovert who had no time for introspective probing; therefore, the unexpected surge of emotion that swept through him as he looked down at her baffled him. Unnerved him too. He was about to back away when she whispered anxiously, "Do you think I'm losing my mind?"

And instead of backing away, he took both her hands in his. "I don't think you're losing your mind," he said softly. "I think you're having some sort of anniversary grief reaction. Very normal and quite common, I believe."

She gazed up at him, her eyes shimmering. "Has it ever happened to you?"

"To me? No." He tried and failed to imagine himself trapped in a cycle of tears and panic and hysteria. "But then . . ." He frowned thoughtfully. "I've never suffered the kind of loss you have. In fact, I've never suffered any sort of losses at all."

It was true, he realized, reflecting upon the thought with some amazement. He'd never experienced the loss of a loved one. His family consisted of his parents, both of whom were alive and well. His sexual relationships had ended when he wanted them to end, precluding the misery of a romantic rejection. His school and medical career was a stellar record of one success after another.

"Just minor losses," he added, almost to himself. "Like losing the softball game today." He remembered his anger and dejection upon that loss and felt a slow flush suffuse his neck. How childish to get so worked up over something so trivial! He felt like a foolish, overgrown adolescent and he didn't care for the feeling at all.

To banish the uncomfortable insight, he sprang into action. He reached into the car and half lifted her out of it. "Come on, we're going inside."

Her legs were shaky and she stumbled slightly on the pavement. Jason scooped her up in his arms and started toward the house. Laura clutched him, gasping, as her feet left the ground. It was oddly disorienting to be carried, to be in motion and completely powerless. Nervously, she turned her face into the curve of his shoulder.

It was a major mistake, Laura acknowledged dizzily to herself. Her lips were almost touching the hard, tanned column of his neck. The enticing male scent of him filled her nostrils, sensually drugging her. She could feel his shoulder muscles bunch as he turned in the doorway, and she was shiveringly aware of his big, warm hand on her bare thighs.

The Roman shades were shut against the late evening sun, leaving the long, spacious living room cool and shadowed. Jason set her down on a plush U-shaped caramel-colored sofa which was soft and deep and so long it spanned the length of the wall. Laura's eyes flickered to the oversized white cushions, as soft and fluffy as marshmallows, that lay in front of the big stone fireplace. The white carpet beneath had the thickest pile she had ever seen. Everything in the room looked up-to-the-minute expensive, untouched and unlived-in.

Her eyes widened warily. This place didn't look like a home, at least not her concept of a home, with practical rugs and long-lasting traditional furniture and family photos scattered about. It looked like a showpiece from a decorator magazine; a media image of the successful yuppie's home.

She watched Jason slide a disc into his compact disc player and a soothing swell of music filled the room, the sound as exquisitely perfect as the CD ads promised. He got out a crystal decanter and splashed an evil-looking liquid into a small stemmed glass. "Here." He handed it to her. "Drink this down."

Laura stiffened. "What is it?"

"Port." He took a whiff and and grimaced. "One of my patients—an elderly man who'd fractured his pelvis—gave it to me for 'fixing him up,' as he put it. You need something bracing and I keep very little hard liquor around. If you don't want the port, a shot of hundred-proof Wild Turkey will have to do. Another token of appreciation from another patient."

Laura shuddered. "I don't want anything to drink."

"You need it, Laura." He held the glass to her lips. "Drink it."

"I don't want it." The fumes made her eyes burn and she shrank back against the sofa cushions. "Why are you trying to force it on me?" Her eyes darted wildly around the room. The soft music, the muted light, the big, wide sofa . . .

Suddenly it all fit. This wasn't a home, it was a lair! Carefully arranged and staged by a modern-day wolf for high-tech seduction. "Are you trying to make me drunk?" she demanded breathlessly. Her heart began to slam violently against her ribs.

He was standing above her, towering above her, looking very big and very powerful. Sudden fear slashed through her. How much did she really know about Jason Fletcher? She'd heard some gossip about him during his absence and it all had to do with his love-'em-and-leave-'em reputation. What if—

"For heaven's sake, I'm not trying to get you drunk!" Jason said indignantly. "I'm trying to help you, you little idiot. I assure you, I have no designs on your body. How could I? Those unisex shirt and shorts render you utterly shapeless. It's hardly an outfit to inspire lust in a man." Let alone Jason Fletcher, a bona fide connoisseur of women, he added silently.

"I'm sorry." Laura chewed her lip nervously. "It's just that you hear so much about acquaintance rape these days. And I—I've never been in this situation before . . . alone in a place with a man that I don't know very well."

"Well, it's a first for me too." Jason scowled. "My usual choice of companion isn't someone who suspects me of—of *acquaintance rape!*"

Laura stared bleakly at the thick white shag rug. Now, on top of everything else, she had insulted him. If their chances for achieving a professional working relationship looked dim earlier, now they appeared positively nonexistent.

She closed her eyes with a dejected sigh. And saw . . . She jumped to her feet so quickly, she felt light-headed and swayed precariously.

Jason steadied her with one strong arm. "You saw the crash again, didn't you?" He put the glass to her lips and she gulped down the potent liquid. It scalded her throat as she swallowed, but she kept on drinking. She would do anything, anything to wipe the horror of the accident from her mind.

He poured her another glass and she choked that down too. The room began to spin and her fingers closed tightly around his forearm. "Everything is going 'round," she murmured unsteadily.

"As long as it doesn't collide." Jason gently pushed her down onto the sofa. "Relax, Laura. Just let your mind drift." He sat down beside her, holding her hand.

They were both silent for a few minutes. The music from the CD was smooth and soothing. And then Jason began to talk, about his recent trip and about others he had taken, about people he had met and places he had seen, the words almost inconsequential as his deep voice vibrated through her, calming her, keeping the pain and fear at bay.

Laura listened in a dreamy, suspended state of peace. Her eyelids grew heavy and when they fluttered closed, they stayed closed. There were no more horrible images to torment her. She leaned against him, her head dropping to his shoulder.

Jason expelled a sigh of relief. Only then did he realize just how tense he'd been, wondering if Laura would be plagued again by the frightening visions. He sat there for a few minutes, his arm around her, enjoying the peaceful dusk, the music, and the warm feel of Laura against him.

She wasn't asleep, simply relaxed and resting, savoring the tranquility and their closeness as much as Jason.

He forced himself to stand up when he realized how close he was to falling asleep. The long trip and its jet lag, the exertion of the softball game, and the stress of the near-accident had taken their toll. He wanted to climb into bed and sleep for days!

The thought of the ninety-minute drive to and from Farview was paralyzing. "Laura, will you stay here tonight?" he asked softly, stooping to untie and remove her sneakers. "You can sleep here on the couch or in my extra bedroom. I don't think either of us is up to another drive."

Laura reluctantly opened her eyes. "I can't," she mumbled sleepily.

"Of course you can, honey. I'll be in my own bed in my own room, I swear. I'm too beat to try and impress a woman in bed tonight anyway. I just want to sleep."

"Aunt Sally and Uncle George will be worried sick if I don't come home. They're expecting me around ten and if I don't—"

"Look, I'll call them and explain," Jason said desperately. He was too tired to drive around the block, let alone the whole way to Farview. "What's the number?"

Shoeless now, Laura tucked her feet under her and curled into the deep, soft warmth of the sofa. She didn't want this peaceful contentment to end. Every cell in her body protested at the thought of trudging out to the car and enduring the inter-state weekend traffic all the way to Farview.

Jason was standing a few feet away, a cordless phone in his hand. "What's your phone number, honey?"

Automatically, she gave it to him.

Just as reflexively, he dialed the number and within moments a deep male voice came over the line. Jason paused, suddenly aware that he didn't know who he was calling. "Uh, is this Laura's uncle George?" he asked, feeling as gauche as a thirteen-year-old telephoning his first girlfriend.

Uncle George was easy to talk to. And quite eager to talk about Laura. When Jason hung up the phone ten minutes later, he stared at Laura in shocked silence.

She looked so calm and serene, snuggled up on the sofa, her eyelids half closed, the curve of her lovely mouth relaxed in peaceful repose. He should leave her alone, he knew that. But he couldn't, not now. The peculiar urgency churning inside him drove him to cross the room and sit down beside her.

"Laura, your uncle told me that your parents were killed in a head-on collision twenty years ago, when you were just five. He said that you were in the backseat of the car when it happened, shortly before midnight." His voice was husky, his tone urgent. "And that you've always claimed that you remembered nothing of the accident, that you wouldn't even speak of it for years."

Laura sat up straight. The peace had vanished, and she struggled to regain her lost guard. It was difficult. She was too emotionally drained to erect her usual barriers of control. But the prospect of another bout of uncontrollable weeping was threatening enough to make her try. "I don't remember my parents' accident," she insisted. "And I don't know why Uncle George even mentioned it to you."

"He mentioned it because I told him about those flashbacks you've been having. And they *are* flashbacks, Laura. You're finally reliving the night your parents died. It all fits. The backseat, the headlights, the screams and then the terrible silence. Your uncle said a car jumped the median strip and plowed right into your parents' car. They were killed instantly and your sister and brother were injured and unconscious. You were thrown to the floor and suffered a broken shoulder and arm, but were conscious throughout. When the ambulances arrived you told the—"

"I don't remember. I was only five years old. I don't remember any of it."

"Your mind wouldn't allow you to remember because it was too traumatic for a child to deal with. You successfully repressed it for years. But that truck heading for us tonight brought it all back. You're ready to cope with it now, Laura, and—"

"I said I don't remember," she insisted frantically. "How much do *you* remember from when you were five?" She stood up abruptly. "I don't want to talk about something that happened so long ago. I just want to go home."

"I told your uncle that you were spending the night here and he agreed it was a good idea."

Laura scowled fiercely. "You and Uncle George certainly got chummy fast."

"He was concerned about you, Laura, and I always respond to that kind of concern. Laura, your uncle said that he and your aunt have always worried about the way you repressed all and any memories of the accident. He said even as a child you were controlled and guarded, that you've always had trouble expressing emotion. He said he's never seen you cry, Laura. Not even on the day of your fiancé's death."

"I suppose you found that hard to believe since I've done nothing but cry for the past hour or so."

"You have a lot to cry about," Jason said quietly. "Twenty years' worth of grief and tears. You've bottled it up for too long, Laura. It had to come out."

He was still shaken by the tragic tale her uncle had related. Poor little Laura, five years old, a witness to her own orphaning. And then in a terrible twist of fate, to lose her fiancé the same way, on the day they were to have been married.

But Laura had adjusted, endured, triumphed even. Her uncle George's words echoed in Jason's ears. *"From the moment she came to live with us she was the perfect child who grew into the perfect teenager and then the perfect young woman,"* her uncle had said, his voice reflecting both worry and admiration. *"After Danny was killed, she was even the perfect sorrowing survivor. I know it's been a terrible burden for her. Just once her aunt and I would love to see Laura let go and be free."*

"Don't feel sorry for me!"

Laura's voice, sharp and furious, cut through his musing. Jason's eyes widened. The young woman who stood defiantly before him, her hands clenched at her sides, her eyes flashing a brilliant blue-green fire, was neither the pitiful orphaned child nor the tragically widowed bride-to-be he'd been imagining.

"I don't want your pity, dammit!" Laura surprised herself with the mild oath. She never swore.

But then, she'd never allowed herself to become angry enough to need to curse. She was angry now, though. "I don't want anybody to feel sorry for me. I never have."

"I wasn't feeling sorry for you," Jason protested. "I was—uh—trying to empathize with you."

She rolled her eyes in mocking disdain. "How would anyone whose only loss has been one soft-ball game know how to empathize?"

She did have a point, Jason conceded reluctantly. He felt a spark of anger kindle within him. True, he was the adored and only son of a couple who'd denied him nothing; equally true, he'd always gotten whatever he wanted, achieved whatever he'd set out to do. But that didn't mean he was incapable of feeling empathy for this young woman who had suffered so many grievous losses. Did it?

"I can feel empathy if I want to," he insisted. It was just that he usually chose not to. Not this time, though. He really was hurting for Laura.

"Well, I don't want your *empathy*," Laura snapped. "Or your sympathy, either. I don't accept sympathy from anyone. I detest it." She gave her head a violent shake. "All those people saying 'poor little Laura,' expecting me to break, waiting for me to fall apart. Twenty years ago and then again three years ago. Well, it never happened. I wouldn't let it."

"Underneath that quiet exterior, you're a tough little cookie, aren't you?" Jason stared at her, bemused. But then she'd have to be, to have successfully overcome the staggering adversity of having her life shattered by fate, not once but twice.

"Yes, I'm tough," Laura said, glaring back at him. A strange recklessness poured through her, invigorating her, infusing her with a dizzying exhilaration she had never before experienced.

She had never fought with anyone before—not calm, dispassionate Laura. She was always reasonable, rational, and impeccably polite, no matter what she might be feeling. But at this moment, her behavior matched the way she felt. For the first time in twenty years.

She was angry and felt like lashing out and she actually was doing it. She knew her behavior was undoubtedly unreasonable, irrational, and rude, but for the first time she didn't care.

"I'm strong and I always have been," she raged on. "And I don't want—"

" 'I don't want, I don't need,' " Jason mimicked her. "Baby, at this point you're too tightly strung to know what you want or need."

She faced him, her eyes enormous and glittering, a feverish wildness circulating in her veins. "And I suppose you do? Know what I want? What I need?" The words slipped out, challenging him, daring him, spoken by an impetuous, volatile Laura who was a stranger to her normal restrained self. It was as if another person had been cast in the role of Laura Novak and was following a script already written.

"Yes." He stared at her, the heat building within him. The powerful tides of emotion pouring through Laura were affecting him too, sweeping him along like flotsam in a raging flood. "Oh yes, Laura, I do."

His next moves seemed preordained, as inevitable as night following day. There was no choice; perhaps neither of them had had one from the moment they'd met and joined forces on the softball field. Certainly not since the blue pickup truck had come speeding down the road at them. For his choice had been to leave her alone. She was not a live-for-the-moment, no-strings-attached Jason Fletcher type. Her choice was to go home, secure in her cocoon of reserve, protected by her unshakable control.

But neither choice had been granted. He was here, wanting her, his body growing hard with desire. And she was with him, her control torpedoed by the hurricane force of her own emotions.

"This is what you want." Jason's hands fastened around her hips to draw her slowly, inexorably toward him. He pressed her into the cradle of his heat, moving against her hot and hard as his blood thundered through his veins. "This is what you need." Something was slipping away from him, the ability to detach and distance himself from emotional needs and demands, both his and hers. "Me."

Laura felt his power radiate through her and went weak and soft inside. Her heart was thudding, her mind spinning. Her breathing became thick and unsteady. Desire, the force of which she had never known, tore through her, obliterating every emotional block in the walls she'd built to protect herself.

"Am I right, Laura?" Jason's voice was husky and thick and seemed to come from another dimension.

She slowly lifted her eyes to his. The scorching anger that had exploded inside her had somehow transformed itself into an equally wild passion. She couldn't think rationally when Jason was looking at her like this; she could only feel and what she felt was a sense of rightness so strong it couldn't be denied.

"Yes," she whispered, letting her arms glide slowly, sensually onto his shoulders. She was operating on pure instinct that directed her fingertips over his hard, smooth-shaven jaw.

"Tell me," he demanded in a whisper, catching her hand and pressing her palm to his lips.

She felt as if she were in a dream as a shimmering liquid heat burned through her, melting her. Throbbing little ripples quivered through her as awakening passion combined with the undiscovered sensuality suddenly blossoming to life within her. "It's you," she murmured huskily, her voice vibrant with wonder. "I want you."

Her words inflamed them both. It was as if

saying them cut the final ties with her old tense, inhibited self. Laura spun giddily out of control, giving herself over completely to the elemental hunger he aroused in her. She had never felt this way before, never experienced the profound need that Jason, and only Jason, had inspired in her. She felt feminine and sensual and free. Free for the first time in her life. Free from the rigid demands and controls she placed on herself, free from the pain and fear of loving and losing.

I want you. The aching feminine need in her voice echoed in his head. His senses were full of her, the warm, supple feel of her skin, the sweet musk of her scent. He hungered for the taste of her, wanting her mouth with a desperation he couldn't match in his memory.

His lips touched hers, lightly at first, nibbling at them, tantalizing her until she moaned softly and opened her mouth in sensual invitation. And then his mouth covered hers, hot and hungry, fierce in its demand. His hand came up to cover her breast and she could feel the heat and strength of it burn through her T-shirt and bra. A jolt of sensual electricity shuddered through her as his fingers found her nipple which was already hard and tight beneath the cloth.

Her arms tightened around his neck and her fingers threaded restlessly through the thickness of his hair. Her tongue slipped into his mouth and she rubbed it provocatively against his, kissing him with a hunger and intensity that would have shocked her usual too-controlled self. But she clung to him, trembling with passion, forgetting everything as he kissed her the way she wanted to be kissed, *needed* to be kissed, deep and hard and demanding.

Jason crushed her against him, running his hands over the slender curves of her body, feeling her, learning that the loose fit of her clothes disguised a sweetly feminine and thoroughly enticing figure. Her breasts were small but full, her waist narrow, her hips softly rounded. And she was wound around him, clinging to him in frank and total surrender which was as seductive and irresistible as the tempestuous desire that flared so swiftly, so fiercely between them.

He felt as if he'd stepped into another world where all the usual rules didn't apply. The women he chose were invariably sexually sophisticated and his relationships with them were physically satisfying but superficial. He didn't concern himself with their emotions, nor did he expect to have his own feelings engaged.

It was different with Laura, though. He'd known that before he'd touched her, and having her in his arms verified it. He was reeling under the force of emotions he couldn't control; he felt possessive and protective of her. Tenderness, compassion, affection, and admiration—all these strange feelings he'd never experienced with the ladies in his life—erupted within him. Tonight he was breaking all his own rules, but nothing had ever seemed more right.

Four

"Laura, I want to make love to you," Jason whispered against her ear.

"Yes." Laura's voice sounded throaty and far away. She leaned heavily against him, her head tilted back, giving his lips full access to the soft white curve of her neck.

A great shudder of desire racked his body and Laura felt the convulsive movements and moaned. His mouth moved on hers again, and they kissed and kissed, as if they were lovers who had been parted for many years and were at last reunited.

And then he was carrying her through the living room and up a carpeted stairway to a high-ceilinged bedroom with a sloped roof. It was definitely a masculine room, decorated in dark shades of red, navy, and off-white. A thick quilt, striped with the three colors, had been carelessly pulled over the navy-and-white pin-striped sheets, and pillows were scattered across the bed.

Still holding her in his arms, Jason swept off the top sheet and quilt with a deft one-handed motion, then placed her on the mattress. He came down on top of her and their mouths met hungrily in a deep voluptuous kiss.

Laura arched into him, her breasts swollen and sensitive as they rubbed the hardness of his chest, her hips fitting snugly against his. His thigh was hard and high between hers, pressing against her vulnerable feminine softness. When she moved, the heat and pressure of that solid masculine thigh sent shock waves of pleasure rolling through her.

She clung to him, kissing him as hungrily as he was kissing her. When he lifted her slightly to take off her T-shirt, she mindlessly raised her arms to facilitate its removal. His experienced fingers unclasped the clip of her practical white cotton bra before she could blink.

At that moment a draft of cool air from the air-conditioning vent swept over her and she shivered. A sudden flash of awareness jolted her out of her passion-induced daze. She was in bed, half naked, with a man she'd met only hours earlier. It was incredibly un-Lauralike behavior, a one-hundred-eighty-degree turn from her usual caution and control.

Her eyes darted to his face and she saw him gazing at her bare breasts. Laura's breath caught in her throat at the rapt look in his eyes.

With a tenderness that surprised him more than her, he brushed his lips along the delicate line of her collarbone, following it from her shoulder to her throat. She suddenly seemed so small and young and vulnerable. Her skin was soft and tantalizingly scented. A mixture of desperation and anticipation surged through him.

It was dangerous, this rush of feelings she evoked in him. He wanted her too much and with a hunger he didn't understand. Today had been a strange day with a myriad of strong emotions and unexpected insights. Was this intense need for her simply a matter of timing? Of her happening to be with him when he was in an emotionally vulnerable state?

He gazed down into her big, jewel-colored eyes. Laura quivered and her lips, swollen from his kisses, looking sensuously bee-stung, parted slightly. She murmured his name and a fresh wave of passion swelled within him. For whatever reason, he found her irresistible. "I have to taste you," he said in a low, gritty voice, then lowered his head to her breast.

The warm, wet feel of his mouth on her nipple sent Laura careening back into sensual fantasyland. She didn't want to be careful and controlled; this was *Jason*, not merely a man she'd met today. He was Jason and being with him gave her a feeling of the supreme rightness of it. This heated, excited desire and the reckless happiness he inspired were too overpowering to be reasoned away. It was as if she'd been merely existing until Jason had taken her into his arms and then she had come to life. . . .

For the first time Laura understood all those fairy tales about the princess being awakened by the prince's kiss. As a gravely serious child who'd never dared to let her mind roam into the carefree, impractical world of fantasy, she'd always found those tales foolish and incomprehensible. But now . . .

She shut her eyes tight and moaned with enjoyment as Jason's tongue laved her sensitive nipple, pulling it into his mouth in a sucking motion, then gently, erotically nipping at it. Now she understood the difference between existence and being truly alive. Snow White, Sleeping Beauty— they didn't seem so foolish and incomprehensible after all.

"You have beautiful breasts, Laura," Jason said in a husky tone. He caressed them with his hands, with his mouth. They were rounded and white and firm with dusky pink tips taut and tingling with arousal.

"Oh, Jason." Laura felt a wave of exquisite pleasure sweep through her. She stared down at the erotic sight of his dark head against her breast and threaded her fingers through the thickness of his hair, holding him to her, stroking him lovingly. Her eyes misted as an overwhelming tenderness surged through her. She felt more feminine than she'd ever felt in her life; she'd never experienced this aching need to give and give of herself.

Jason's hands glided to her waist to sensually investigate the slender curves of it, then lowered to her stomach and over the contours of her hips. His caresses were slow and thorough, almost leisurely. Laura found herself arching and squirming under his practiced hands.

Jason watched her feminine, sensual movements and saw the warm flush spread from her breasts to her cheeks, and his body grew even harder in response to her growing excitement. He easily untied the drawstring of her shorts and pushed them over her hips, then removed them with one final sweep. His fingers traced the waistband of her demure white cotton panties, dipping below to explore the hollow of her navel with his thumb.

Laura's breath caught and she closed her eyes as a flash of sharp heat uncurled deep within her, piercing her to the core. She flexed her knee, opening herself to him in silent invitation. Rhythmic spirals of sensation made her want to twist languorously under his touch.

Jason laughed softly, the sound thrillingly sensual. "Do you know how sexy you are?" he asked before groaning with pleasure. "You're so responsive, so uninhibited and sexually honest. Sweet Laura, you let me know exactly how I make you feel."

His words of praise, growled in that rough, warm voice, made her glow. She felt as if she were swirling into a deep, mysterious whirlpool, slipping slowly under the blissful currents as Jason's hands moved over her.

Her panties formed a thin cloth barrier between her burning skin and his big, warm hands. Laura's heartbeat thundered in her ears as he methodically explored the firm roundness of her buttocks and her flat, taut stomach through the soft white cotton. His sensual search seemed to go on for an eternity.

"Jason, please," she whimpered, disconcerted by the force of the melting, yearning urgency which gripped her. She wanted to feel his hands on her bare thighs, between them.

The hot feelings sizzling inside her were so new and almost unbearably exciting. She ached . . . and she wanted . . .

"Yes, sweetheart." He breathed against her neck, taking sensuous, hungry little nibbles of the creamy skin there. "Tell me. Let me know what you want. Let me hear what you're feeling."

With a wild little cry, Laura captured his mouth with hers and kissed him passionately, telling him with actions instead of words of the intensity of her desire and need for him. Jason responded at once to her hungry demand. He pulled down her panties and slid his hand between her legs.

Laura groaned as his fingers tangled in the soft downy triangle, then gently probed the hot, moist feminine fire which parted sweetly for him. As he eased into her, he felt the soft flesh tighten to hold him within.

Her response washed over him like liquid lightning. His breathing grew ragged. He wanted her with a violence that shocked him; her need, her physical *demand* for him was a potent lure. Gone was his self-control and with it the choreographed moves with which he mastered his passion. His emotions were raging wildly, and his surrender was as complete as hers.

His hands shaking, he tugged at his shirt, and

Laura knelt up on the bed to help him jerk it over his head. He tossed it to the floor and a few feverish seconds later the rest of his clothes landed there as well.

For a moment, Laura gazed at the nude splendor of him, the rigid, well-defined pectoral muscles, the powerful biceps, and hard, flat stomach. She reached out to touch him, her eyes wide with wonder. "It would have made learning anatomy so much easier if only the nursing schools had a model like you to study," she said, smiling with warm humor and admiration.

Jason grinned broadly, although he knew he wasn't supposed to feel like laughing out loud when he was in bed with a naked woman. He'd always treated lovemaking with the same serious consideration he gave to sports, and spontaneous bursts of laughter simply didn't fit.

But Laura delighted him, filling him with a lighthearted happiness that he'd never experienced while following the guidelines he'd set for making love. Although Jason played hard, he could never be described as playful. Yet he felt that way now as he caught Laura's hand and pressed it to his lips.

"Did you have trouble with anatomy, Miss Novak?" he asked, his gray eyes teasing.

She groaned. "It was the worst! And when they gave us those dead cats to dissect, I thought I'd die right there on the spot."

"Laura!" Jason made a sound that was something of a combined laugh and yelp of protest. "May I remind you that this is neither the time nor the place to bring up such a repulsive subject."

"Does it turn you off, Jason?" She managed one credible look of puzzled innocence before dissolving into laughter.

"Does it look like I'm turned off, Laura?"

Her gaze followed his, dropping to his aroused manhood which throbbed with virile potency.

Laura swallowed. Still holding her hand, Jason guided it to the powerful shaft. "Does it *feel* like I'm turned off, Laura?"

Her fingers closed around him intimately and their eyes met and held. "Laura!" he murmured jaggedly as she caressed him with a hesitant sweetness that maddened him. He couldn't stop himself from thrusting in counterpoint to her motions.

An instant later, Laura found herself lying flat on her back, pinned beneath the heavy warm weight of his body. He caught her wrists and pulled them above her head, locking them together with his hand.

Laura stared into the smoldering gray depths of his eyes. "Don't you want me to touch you?" she whispered, confused. "Don't you like—"

Jason silenced her with a long, deep kiss.

When he finally lifted his mouth, his voice was a husky growl. "Lord, yes, I like to feel your hands on me. So much that if I let you keep touching me that way, my sexy beautiful baby, it would be all over in seconds. And that's not the way I want it to be for either of us."

Laura blushed. "I—I'm kind of new at all of this." She shivered a little, running the tip of her tongue over her lower lip in a nervous gesture that he found inexplicably entrancing.

"How new?" he asked softly.

She wanted to touch him. Since her hands were still chained above her head, she rubbed her slim leg along the hair-roughened length of his. Jason watched her sinuous movements, his eyes dilating with passion. His free hand moved over her in long, slow caresses, enticing and arousing.

"I was in no hurry to have sex," she said dreamily. "Luckily for us both, I suppose, Danny wasn't either. We agreed to wait—until we were married."

Her wedding night would have been three years ago tonight; the thought floated across her mind. Missing was the pain that she'd have expected to accompany it. Also missing was any sense of guilt for lying here with Jason. An image of Danny's smiling face rose hazily in her mind's eye, before fading mistily away. Danny had loved life and he'd loved her. He would never begrudge her the chance to find love. Why, he would encourage her!

Laura gazed into Jason's eyes. His hand had stilled but rested possessively on her stomach. "You're telling me that you're a virgin?" he asked quietly. "That I—I'm the first?"

"Does it bother you?"

He cleared his throat. "It scares the hell out of me. Why, Laura? Why have you waited so long to go to bed with a man? And don't say it was because you were in no hurry to have sex. You're so sexy and passionate and responsive. You practically come apart in my hands when I touch you."

She inched closer and curled herself into him, so that their bodies touched intimately. "I never felt sexy or passionate or responsive until you made me feel that way, Jason. I—I feel as if I've opened a door to a whole new world today, and in that world is a whole new me."

He was touched by her honesty. He knew he'd never been the sort of man to give; for years he'd taken, sometimes selfishly, sometimes thoughtlessly. It would be different with Laura, he knew, and he wasn't quite sure how to handle it. The fact that he wasn't running for his life—or more aptly, his carefree bachelor lifestyle—spoke volumes in itself.

Right now he was beyond analyzing or rationalizing. He was too passionately involved to think beyond the moment. He released her hands and gathered her into his arms. "I won't hurt you," he promised, and his lips brushed hers in a gentle kiss.

Laura heard a moan and knew it was hers as a fresh spasm of desire ripped through her. She pressed herself tightly against him, opening her mouth in hot promise beneath his.

Hunger exploded within him and he cupped her shoulders and tried to hold her away from him. "Laura, baby, I'm trying to go slowly. I want to be gentle but—"

She wriggled from under his hands and pushed close to him, locking herself to him by wrapping her arms and legs around him. "I don't want you to go slow," she said huskily. "I don't want you to be gentle." She felt wild and daring and fiercely eager to please him. And to sample the full extent of these new, thrilling pleasures he had introduced her to. "Kiss me, Jason. Kiss me hard."

He was only too happy to oblige her. The kiss was hard and deep and intimately rapacious. He slipped his hand between her thighs and stroked her, making her gasp at the unbelievably pleasurable spirals of heat which radiated from the melting center of her.

"Honey, I can't wait any longer." His voice was thick with urgency. He was shaking with the effort to hold back. "You're ready for me, baby," he breathed with soft satisfaction. She quivered and sighed. "So very ready."

He moved between her legs, lifting her hips to receive him, then surged into her with a single, swift movement. Laura tensed at the sudden stab of pain and clenched her teeth tightly together to keep from crying out.

Atop her, inside her, Jason braced himself on his elbows and stared down at her. "This is no time to exercise control, Laura," he said hoarsely. "If it hurts, let it out. For heaven's sake, don't play the perfect sacrificial virgin."

"I—I don't know what you mean."

"I mean that I know all about your determination to be perfect, Laura. Your uncle George told me he's never known you to make a wrong move. So here you are, with me inside you, wondering why it isn't like all those love scenes you've read about in books, but attempting to do what you think is expected of you anyway."

He'd read her so well. Laura gripped his shoulders so tightly that she feared she might mark him with her nails, professionally short though they were. "It hurt a little at first," she conceded.

Jason's mouth curved into a wry smile. From what her uncle had said, the need to be perfect was deeply ingrained in Laura. "And that's all you'll own up to," he murmured, feathering his lips along the smooth curve of her throat. Affection and understanding surged through him and he didn't bother to ponder how or why he understood her so well. Or liked her so much. He just did and it seemed so very right.

He kissed the curve of her shoulder. "Relax, darling. It's going to be good for you, I promise. You're going to enjoy it and want it again and again. Want *me* again and again," he amended. It seemed important to clarify that point.

Once more, as in the car earlier, his soothing words served as an almost mesmerizing balm. As Laura relaxed, her rigid muscles unlocked. The uncomfortable sense of being stretched and invaded disappeared, replaced by a hot honeyed pleasure that made her sigh.

"Jason, it's good," she whispered, clinging to him, running her hands over the long hard length of his back. She felt no shyness or inhibitions with him. She could tell him anything. "You're right, I am enjoying it!"

Jason made a husky sound that was half laugh and half groan. "So am I, baby. You're so hot and tight, Laura. I've never felt anything like this. You're perfect."

"There's that word again." Laura surprised herself with the small joke. As a dedicated perfectionist, this was the first time she'd ever found humor in the quest for perfection.

They laughed together. And kissed. And soon the room was filled with the sensuous sounds of a man and a woman making love. Rustling bed covers. Whispers and moans and sighs.

Jason moved within her and Laura reveled in the fullness of him inside her. He filled an emptiness she wasn't even aware of, made her half of a perfect whole. She gave herself up to the enthralling excitement that built and built between them, taking them higher and higher, his desire spurring hers, hers inciting his in a pulsating, exquisite cycle of giving and taking.

As the ultimate pleasure exploded through him, Jason called out Laura's name just at the moment that delicious convulsions of ecstasy erupted deep within her. The long, shattering release transported them to the heights of rapture where they soared, united in body and spirit, in a world beyond time and place where they were transformed and transfigured by the intensity of their union.

They lay together in the cool dark silence, their bodies still joined in the wild, sweet aftermath of their climax.

"This can't be real," Jason said, his voice thick and dazed. The emotional force of their lovemaking was beyond anything he had ever experienced. Laura engaged and involved him on every level; for the first time in his life he had given all and held nothing back. He felt drained and utterly replete, unable to move or even think. The total emotional and physical catharsis coupled with his latent case of jet lag made staying awake an impossibility.

"It's a dream," Laura agreed drowsily. She too was drifting into sleep on a wave of supreme content. "And you're my dream lover, Jason." It was wonderful, this blissful floating sensation, this joyous feeling of total freedom. Dreamily, she kissed his shoulder, his neck, tasting the salty sweat, savoring the sensual weight of him.

"I'm crushing you, baby," Jason mumbled sleepily, moving to roll aside.

"No!" Laura clung to him. "Don't leave me yet." She held him within her with a reflexive movement deep inside her body. "You feel so good like this. I don't want to let you go."

This really was a dream, Jason thought foggily. Had he ever known a woman as sensually honest and open as Laura? He kissed her tenderly, his mind drifting in an insensate haze. "I'm not going to leave you, sweetheart. I'll never leave you."

They slept.

It was much later, and Laura was dreaming of Jason, dreaming that she lay snuggled into the hard, warm curve of his body, dreaming that his big hands were caressing her breasts. Slowly, her eyelids opened. The room was completely dark and the red light from the digital clock gave off an eerie other-worldly glow. The numbers read 2:16.

And then she realized that she'd been in that odd state of half dreaming and half wakefulness. For she really was lying snuggled in the hard, warm curve of his body and his big hands cupped her breasts, caressing them, fondling the soft flesh, running his thumbs over the hardening nipples.

She murmured his name.

"I want you, Laura." His voice was soft and low against her ear. "Come to me, baby."

She felt his hard, naked strength thrusting against her and response quivered through her. Half asleep in the darkness, she glided in and out of an erotic dream, moving sinuously against him, moaning softly.

Jason's hand moved between her legs, caressing and seeking. Her eyes closed heavily, and she gave herself up to the luscious waves of pleasure rippling through her. He sheathed himself deep inside her and she felt no pain at all, just the sweet shock of being filled with an overflowing pleasure.

She wasn't sure if she were awake or dreaming and she didn't care as her body matched the primitive sensual rhythm of his. There were only the two of them in this private dark world, flowing together in a sensuous spiral of desire and fulfillment.

It happened again and again during the hours that followed. Laura and Jason revolved in a cycle of passion and sleep, arousing and satisfying each other as Saturday night blended into Sunday morning. It wasn't until the afternoon was fading into night once again that the need for such a mundane thing as food surfaced.

"I think I'm starving," Jason said to Laura as his stomach growled in protest. "Between you and the jet lag, my belly doesn't know what day it is, let alone when I had my last meal."

Laura lay sprawled over him, satiated and languorous from their latest explosive, passionate union. It was the first time she had been on top, and her body was still quivering with sensuous, orgasmic aftershocks.

She had lost track of the day and the time and everything else that didn't pertain to being in bed with Jason. Her reality had narrowed to include him and only him. She didn't have to eat or drink or even think. Especially not think. Dreamily, she buried her face in the hollow of his shoulder and let her mind drift away.

"Take a little nap, honey." Jason gently shifted her off him and tucked the quilt around her. "I'll rustle us up something to eat."

Obediently, Laura rolled over and snuggled into the pillows with a sigh.

The house was still and dim in the twilight. Moving in a sleep-induced, passion-induced, jet-lag-induced fog, Jason stumbled into the kitchen and peered inside the refrigerator. He was mildly astonished to find it almost empty, then recalled that he'd been away for six weeks and had used up or given away all the perishable items before leaving for Belfast.

He tried the freezer and triumphantly pulled out a big dish of frozen ravioli, homemade for him before he'd left for Ireland by Rita, the sultry flight attendant. He and Rita had an easy, casual relationship—if even that loosely interpreted word could describe their occasional, pleasant forays into the bedroom. When she'd confided her hopes of marrying a senior pilot, Jason had wished her luck. He'd even offered her some advice on how to snare the pilot of her dreams the last time they'd been together—and she'd made him this batch of cheese-and-meat ravioli in a gesture of thanks and goodwill. He found nothing incongruous about sharing the meal with Laura. Rita seemed like a figment of his imagination, some hazy figure from someone else's past. Laura was his only reality.

There was a bottle of sparkling red wine chilling in the refrigerator, an inexpensive brand more closely related to soda pop than wine, but Jason, no connoisseur, didn't care. Twenty minutes later, he carried the microwave-heated ravioli, the wine, two glasses, and two forks into the bedroom.

"Dinner is served," he announced and with a flourish sat down on the bed with the meal.

A languorous Laura rolled onto her side and opened her eyes. He speared a ravioli with a fork and offered it to her. "We're eating in here?" She looked bemused. "Right out of the dish?"

"It's energy efficient. Why bother with plates? Look at the dishwashing time this saves." He moved the fork closer to her lips. "Come on, sweetness, eat your dinner—or breakfast or brunch or supper or whatever this meal is called."

She sat up a little and allowed him to feed her. It did not seem out of the ordinary for her to be eating naked in bed after twenty-four hours of continual lovemaking. No, it didn't seem the least unusual to this sensuous new creature who seemed to have taken possession of Laura Novak.

She picked up a fork and fed a ravioli square to him. He chewed it as he opened the bottle of wine. "My brother doesn't approve of wine with twist-off tops," she remarked, watching him. "His wine-tasting club would collectively cringe."

"Yeah, yeah. Those fancy wine buffs call this *faux* wine." He topped each of the two glasses with the fizzing cherry-red liquid. "But I'll tell you a deep, dark secret: To me, it doesn't taste all that different from the stuff they sell for ninety bucks a bottle. Sometimes it tastes better."

He handed her a glass and she drank it down thirstily. "I think you're right," she decided and held out her glass. "More *faux* wine, please."

Jason obliged. "Careful, little girl," he warned with a lascivious leer. "I just might be trying to get you drunk so I can have my wicked way with you."

"That's what I thought when you offered me that awful port, remember?" Laura drained her second glass. She was thirstier than she'd realized.

"I remember." He smiled at her and she smiled back. "That seems like a million years ago," he said softly, warm waves of desire and affection lapping through him as he gazed into her smiling blue-gray-green eyes. She had the most unusually beautiful eyes. He felt the stirrings of arousal tightening his body.

"It *was* a million years ago," Laura whispered, reaching out to stroke the stubble-roughened line of his jaw. The appeal of the unshaven male, popularized by television antiheroes, had always eluded her until now. Jason looked sexy and excitingly virile. Her blood caught fire. Her head was spinning from the wine, from the mercuric forceful desire that raged through her as she looked at him, as she touched him. "It was in another universe, in another lifetime." Her eyes, wide and expressive, told him how much she wanted him.

It took Jason all of ten seconds to clear the empty dish, bottle, and glasses from the bed. And then he reached for Laura, pulling her tightly into his arms. "What kind of spell have you cast over me, you little sorceress?" he asked, only half joking. "It's never been like this with anyone. I can't get enough of you." With a sensual groan, his mouth came down fiercely on hers.

Laura breathed a small sigh of contentment and melted against him. It was exactly the same for her. She couldn't get enough of him, either. And if she were a sorceress, then he was a sorcerer for he'd cast an identical spell upon her.

Five

Physically and emotionally exhausted, replete from the food and wine, their passion sated, Jason and Laura slept straight through the next twelve hours. When Jason opened his eyes at ten o'clock on Labor Day morning, the languid, sensual torpor which had held him in thrall during the erotic dreamlike atmosphere of the weekend had evaporated.

Replacing it was the cold, harsh chill of reality. Slowly, Jason turned his head to look at Laura, who lay on her left side in the middle of the bed, so close to him that he had to cling to the edge of the mattress to avoid touching her. She looked simultaneously innocent and sensual in the cloudy morning light. She had snuggled deep under the covers and he resisted the urge to fling them back and gaze at her rosy nakedness.

A hot shaft of desire spun through him and his pulses raced. With alarm. *What had happened to him this weekend?* He'd brought Laura to his home to calm and reassure her but somehow his good intentions had gone awry and they'd ended up in bed! A hundred torrid memories washed over him as he stared down at Laura's sleeping form. The incredibly intimate things they had done, the ardent impassioned things they'd said. He flushed. Had that man really been Jason Fletcher?

Feeling as if his skin were on fire, he swiftly, purposefully, left the bedroom and headed to the shower, leaving behind the alluring sight of Laura, nude and sleeping in his bed.

He stared at his reflection in the mirror. Looking back at him was the Jason Fletcher he knew, not the tender, amorous lover who'd spent the better part of the weekend making love to a sweet little virgin, the kind of woman who would call the physical fireworks between them "love" instead of what they really were, great sex. The kind of woman he'd spent his adult life avoiding because he wasn't in the market to meet her particular set of demands: the promises of never-ending devotion and fidelity, marriage, and kiddies.

Jason broke out in a cold sweat, even as the hot needles of the shower spray beat down on him. *Kiddies!* In his mind's eye, he saw himself discreetly reach for the foil-packeted condom before he made love to Laura for the first time. But after that . . .

Erotic images tumbled, kaleidoscope-style, through his mind. There wasn't a condom in any of them. He shut his eyes tightly and groaned aloud. *Dear Lord, what if he'd made her pregnant!* The shampoo bottle he was holding fell from his suddenly nerveless fingers and landed on his foot. It felt like a rock had smashed his toe and he uttered a searing curse. And then another. He cursed the shampoo, his throbbing big toe, and primarily himself for being so incredibly, so inexplicably, so uncharacteristically stupid to make love to a woman without any regard for precautions.

His hand was shaking so badly that he cut himself shaving twice, another unheard-of lapse for Jason Fletcher. Since the first time he'd made love at the rambunctious, hormonally driven age of sixteen, he'd been careful to protect himself and his partner. He'd practiced safe sex for years before it became a catchphrase. He'd never had a sexually transmitted disease—or a pregnant girlfriend.

As Laura had been a virgin, he knew his health was still safe. The razor slipped from his hand and fell into the basin of the sink. *But what about a baby?*

Even though he was thirty-eight years old—today! *Happy Birthday, Daddy?*—he'd yet to experience the so-called biological urge of generativity. He'd never felt the need to populate the world with little Fletchers. Though he hadn't actively ruled it out, he'd relegated fatherhood to the future . . . the future so distant that it had yet to arrive.

Until now? Jason towel-dried his hair with punishing force. He was seldom around children, had very little experience with them. There was his pediatrics rotation in medical school, of course, but he knew he oughtn't base his attitude toward children on the sick youngsters he'd met during that time. Nobody, kids included, was at their best while sick and in pain as were the children on the pediatrics floor of the hospital. That they all tended to shriek with horror when anyone in a white coat approached them—and as a medical student, he'd been required to wear that white coat—had been disconcerting in the extreme, though.

He thought about his friend Casey Flynn, once a freewheeling bachelor like himself, now a very married husband and father. He remembered the first time Case had proudly placed his little daughter Shannon in her "Uncle Jason's" arms. She'd howled and spit up all over his new tie. Jason grimaced. He had not been enchanted. In fact he'd been delighted to turn the baby over to her devoted daddy.

But what if he were the daddy?

Lost in the throes of his anxiety attack was Laura herself, the responsive sensual lover who had given herself so generously and deliciously. The natural rapport between them and the dynamic sexual bonds they'd forged were overshadowed by this blitzkrieg of trepidation and alarm.

One minute, Jason berated himself as a sexual predator who'd ruthlessly seduced the helpless young innocent he had intended to comfort. The next, his perspective abruptly shifted and he saw her as an irresistibly tempting siren who'd lured him into her trap with seductive maneuvers so subtle that an open good sport like himself hadn't stood a chance.

But no matter which scenario he considered, regardless of who was victim or villain, the awful truth was that he'd taken a foolish risk with enormous consequences. Jason Fletcher, perennial winner, successful and acclaimed champion of his own destiny, had just handed over his potential freedom and peace of mind to a woman he'd known less than forty-eight hours.

Laura came awake gradually, opening her eyelids slowly, then closing them again. And then they sprang wide open and she bolted upright. She began to tremble as her senses became wholly attuned to her surroundings. She was naked. The sheets smelled muskily of sweat and sex. According to the bedside clock, it was ten-thirty. It was Monday morning and she'd been in this bed, this bedroom, since Saturday night.

Jason wasn't the only one to plunge from the captivating, erotic abandon of the weekend into the icy grip of reality. For the first time in her life, Laura Novak awakened to face that classically chilling question: *Oh God, what have I done?*

The memories rolled over her, gathering force

and momentum with every beat of her heart. Maybe a better question would be what *hadn't* she done, she decided grimly. She saw herself wantonly moving under Jason, over him, kissing and touching him, brazenly initiating, inviting his own bold kisses and caresses. Her heart thundered in her ears and her whole body was one scalding blush. For as horrified as she was by the audacious memories, she was beginning to become aroused by them as well.

Laura jumped out of bed, unable to sit passively for another second. She could hear the water running in the bathroom and was torn between a desperate desire for a shower and the dread of encountering Jason. Glancing wildly around the room, she spied a robe hanging on the hook inside the partially opened closet door. She snatched it and put it on. The prospect of facing Jason was daunting enough without the additional disadvantage of being nude when doing it.

The sight of their clothes scattered over the floor brought back vivid memories of Jason removing them and tossing them aside, of the enthralling sensual delight of bare skin on skin. Laura clutched the lapels of the black silk robe with her icy fingers, then purposefully tightened the narrow belt. Jason's scent lingered in the silky material, which felt soft and sensuously cool against her heated skin.

Quickly, she gathered her clothes and tried to smooth and fold them. It seemed unreal. She'd gone to bed with a man she'd known only a few hours—and then spent the rest of the weekend there!

And not just any man. Oh no, she had to go and choose one of the doctors with whom she would be working daily, one of the influential powers-that-be in the orthopedics department. And not a particularly discreet one, if all that jovial gossip about him was to be believed.

Laura blanched. During the two weeks she'd worked in orthopedics, she'd been treated to a number of Dr. Fletcher tales. Half of them dealt with his prowess as an orthopedic surgeon and a caring, concerned physician; the other half celebrated his prowess as a free-spirited rogue with women whose lines and technique were reportedly fail-safe. She flinched. His reputation was deserved and secure—his lines and technique had been extraordinarily effective with her too.

Was she doomed to star in the next round of hospital gossip, Laura wondered, her stomach roiling. She pictured Jason regaling his admiring colleagues with tales of his latest conquest—the new head nurse on orthopedics. She knew all about the speed and efficiency of hospital grapevines; within moments of his boast, the news would be circulating throughout the Hospital Center that Laura Novak had left the picnic and gone directly to Jason Fletcher's bed.

Laura thought of her professional reputation, which would most definitely not be enhanced by the tale. She was well aware of the old-fashioned, unfair double standard still existing in the medical world. A doctor could sleep with as many women as he could handle, but let a nurse get herself gossiped about and she was branded a tramp, an object of gleeful speculation, not to be taken seriously, especially by the doctors doing the speculating.

And Laura took nursing very seriously; nursing was all that mattered to her. It filled her life. It was all she had. Applying for the position of head nurse had been a monumental step for her. It had meant leaving the safety of Farview Memorial and taking on the challenges of a far more demanding position. And ultimately, when she'd gotten the job, it had meant leaving the shelter of her aunt and uncle's home because she knew that eventually she would have to move closer to her new hospital.

After the three years spent recovering from the loss of Danny and all their dreams, she thought she'd finally been ready to move on; now she was filled with self-doubt. She thought she knew herself so well, but doing something as foolhardy and reckless as jumping into bed with Jason Fletcher turned her into a dangerous enigma unto herself.

Lost in the throes of her anxiety attack was Jason himself, the virile, thoughtful lover who had so passionately transformed her from girlish virgin to sensual woman. The natural rapport between them and the dynamic sexual bonds they'd forged were overshadowed by this onslaught of shame and consternation.

She could only condemn herself for sleeping with a man she'd just met. Jason Fletcher would never respect her, not professionally or personally. He probably considered her one of the easiest lays he'd ever had. Which was undoubtedly the truth. Hot, hurtful tears filled her eyes.

But Laura had spent nearly twenty years building a facade of steely control and almost reflexively, she drew forth her reserves to pull herself together. *She would not cry.* Crying was what had landed her in this mess to begin with. Marshaling every ounce of willpower she possessed, she blinked back the tears. And just in time, too, for the bathroom door swung open. Laura's heart came to a complete halt, then began beating again at a frantic rate.

Jason emerged from the bathroom, a white bath towel wrapped around his middle, covering him from waist to midthigh. Laura's eyes traveled compulsively over him, lingering on the hard, sensual curve of his mouth, the thick dark mat of hair on his chest. A tide of wanton memories made her blood heat. Memories of the deep, deliciously carnal kisses they'd shared. Of her sensuous discovery of his flat male nipples nestled in the soft wiry mat of hair, of the way he had moaned when she'd explored them with her tongue.

Her knees felt dangerously weak. Laura willed them to support her. She wanted to go to him. His voice, deep and low and husky with desire, echoed in her ears. *I want you, Laura . . . Come to me.* How many times during this romantic lost weekend had he uttered those words and how many times had she eagerly complied? Though she could name every reason why she shouldn't, if he were to open his arms to her, she would fly to his side.

Anticipation and apprehension seared her with equal intensity. Desperate to do something, anything to keep her taut nerves from betraying her, she snatched the neat pile of clothes she'd folded at the foot of the bed and clutched them to her chest, as if they were a lead apron protecting her from penetrating X rays.

The sight of Laura, tousled and sexy in his robe, impacted forcefully on Jason's senses, temporarily obliterating every nascent fear he'd experienced since awakening. He was overwhelmed by a plethora of intense memories, all of them featuring Laura's warmth and loving, giving sensual honesty. It was so natural for him to reach for her and for her to be there. He knew that if she were to come to him at this moment, he would carry her right back to bed and make love to her. Risks, traps, and consequences were irrelevant in comparison to his feelings for her.

For several long moments they stared at each other, waiting. He didn't open his arms to her, although he silently willed her into them. She didn't run into his arms, although she prayed he would give her a signal to do exactly that.

Instead they stood stock-still, as if transfixed, and the moment was lost. Their separate defenses and controls kicked in, overriding their emotional vulnerability and any chance for an impulsive, romantic act.

He didn't respect her; he thought she was a trashy one-night stand, Laura thought, her heart sinking. It was obvious that as far as he was concerned, she'd served her purpose and now he wanted her out.

Here it comes, Jason thought. Her vow of undying love. He braced himself. What if she started to cry when he didn't return it? On Saturday night, he'd proven that he was a sucker when it came to her tears. She had to be as fully aware of that as he was. What if—at this very moment—a tenacious little zygote was busily turning itself into a baby deep inside her body? How could he turn his back on a sobbing, pregnant woman? His color drained.

Laura was the first to break the increasing, unnerving tension of silence. Summoning her entire vast reserves of courage and control, she cleared her throat. "May I use the shower now?" she asked politely.

Jason blinked. And gave his head a slight shake. Had he heard her correctly? Had she really asked to use the shower in the impeccably courteous tones of a well-mannered houseguest? There was no impassioned declaration of love, no tearful admonishments about his lack of same. He stared at her, too stunned to reply.

His silence cut Laura like a knife. He didn't even want her hanging around here long enough to shower! She swallowed the huge lump which lodged perilously in her throat. *I've been through worse than this,* Laura kept thinking. *I didn't cry when Uncle George and Aunt Sally told me Mom and Dad were never coming back. I didn't cry when I saw Danny in his coffin. I'll be damned if I'll cry now, over you, Jason Fletcher.*

She lifted her head and held it high. "I hope you don't mind my borrowing your bathrobe," she said in a cool, albeit shaky, voice. "I'll—take it with me when I leave and have it dry-cleaned."

She was so cool. So cordial. So completely unlike the woman he'd spent the weekend with. Jason felt rage rip through him. He felt a totally irrational urge to shake her until her teeth rattled. She was talking to him the way she talked to everyone else; he'd seen her use the same friendly but slightly detached smile and tone at the picnic. It was her social side. But this weekend, he'd seen another side of her—the playful, passionate, intense, emotional side of her that she showed to no one else. The side of her that she was denying to him now.

"You don't have to bother about having the robe dry-cleaned," he said tightly. "And feel free to use the bathroom. I'm finished in there."

"Thank you." Laura was still so emotionally attuned to him from their shared intimacy that she felt the force of his suppressed rage, and her heart turned to lead in her chest. He hated her. She could feel it. She had to get out of there, away from him and his searing hostility. "I'll call my sister first to take me home," she said quickly, her pulses pounding at every point. "If she leaves now, she should be here soon. . . ."

Her voice trailed off and she made a grab for the telephone, concentrating on pushing the buttons, grateful for an excuse to avoid Jason's steely gray eyes.

"Lianna?" She breathed a silent, thankful prayer that her sister had been the one to answer. "This is Laura. Will you come and pick me up? Please!" she added, on a rising desperate note.

"Sure, I'll pick you up. Where are you?" Lianna sounded slightly confused. Had she ever heard Laura's voice as anything but calm, cool, and collected? Though she was thirteen months younger than Lianna, Laura had taken on the traditional characteristics of sensible, organized older sister years ago. "Where are you, Laura?" Lianna repeated impatiently.

Laura's mouth went dry, as the brutal truth struck. "I—I don't know," she gasped, more to herself than to her sister.

"You don't know where you are?" Lianna repeated incredulously. "Hey, is this really my sister Laura, Princess Perfect of the Novaks?"

Laura covered the mouthpiece of the receiver with her hand and turned to Jason, keeping her eyes carefully averted from him as she asked for his address. It was, she decided, one of the most humiliating moments of her life.

Deadpan, Jason recited the directions to his house and Laura passed them along to Lianna. "Please leave right now," she beseeched her sister.

"Oh, you can count on it," Lianna replied dryly. "I can't wait to get the facts on this case."

Everything was a case to Lianna; she was a policewoman and saw life in terms of cases. And her sister had fine-tuned the policely art of questioning, as Laura well knew. She gritted her teeth and gulped back a groan. Facing Lianna would be almost as difficult as facing Jason this morning.

"There was no need for you to ask your sister to drive the whole way down here," Jason said tightly, purposely focusing on the stripes on the wallpaper. He didn't dare look at Laura. Every time he did, he was torn by conflicting urges to grab her and kiss her or to grab her and make her cry . . . so he'd then have an excuse to comfort her by kissing her?

He couldn't, *wouldn't* do either, he vowed. "I can drive you home."

"No. No, thank you," Laura said with a ghastly social smile. "Lianna doesn't mind. Now if—if you'll excuse me . . ." She bolted to the bathroom and closed the door, locking it with trembling fingers. She couldn't tolerate the taut atmosphere of rejection and regret for a second longer.

She prolonged her stay in the bathroom to coincide with Lianna's arrival. When Jason rapped on the door to say, "A car just pulled into the driveway. A blue Dodge Shadow. Is it your sister's car?" she was fully dressed, her hair neatly combed and partially dry from a vigorous toweling.

"Yes, it is," she said through the door. "I'll be right out."

To Laura's horror, when she entered the living room, Jason and Lianna were standing on opposite sides of it, eyeing each other. Lianna with unconcealed interest, Jason with incredulity. Lianna often had that effect on people meeting her for the first time, especially when she was wearing her vice squad decoy togs, as she was now. Lacy red camisole, tight black leather miniskirt, black suspenders visibly attached to a garter belt holding up seamed black stockings, and eye-popping silver spike heels. Her moussed platinum hair with a pink stripe down the middle, cut in a wild, spiky shag, completed the look of streetwise sleaze.

"*She* is your *sister*?" Jason managed to croak. He was dumbfounded. *Laura's sister was a hooker?*

She could explain, of course, but why bother? Laura thought morosely. She'd been counting on Lianna to remain in the car, so they could make a quick, clean getaway. She should have guessed that her sister would be far too curious to pass up the opportunity to investigate "the case." And to shock Jason Fletcher with her working attire.

"So this is Dr. Jason Fletcher?" Lianna's dark gray-green eyes flicked from Laura to Jason. "The same Dr. Jason Fletcher who called to tell Uncle George that Laura was shook up from a near-accident and would be staying in town with her friend Dana?"

"I never said she was staying with Dana!" Jason protested.

"And I guess you didn't refer to yourself as a nice *old* doctor either?" Lianna asked drolly.

Jason flushed. "Of course not!"

"Uncle George is slightly hard of hearing." Lianna grinned, obviously enjoying herself. "And he has a real talent for filling in the gaps with his own facts. Whatever you told him, he interpreted the story as this: Laura and Dana were returning from the picnic and were almost hit by a car. Laura was very upset and a nice old doc—Uncle George's exact words—called to say that Laura was all right but would be staying in town. With Dana, we all presumed. Just like we presumed the nice old doc was a septuagenarian. Looks like we were wrong all the way around."

"Lianna, let's go." Laura crossed the room and caught her sister's elbow to try to propel her out the door.

"Go? Now?" Lianna feigned disappointment. "I wanted to stick around and get acquainted with the nice old doc here." She turned to Jason with a cheeky grin. "You must be quite a guy, Doc. This is the first time I've ever had to retrieve my little sister from a weekend fling. I'd like to—"

"Lianna, stop it," Laura said in a desperate whisper. She gave her sister's arm a pull and jerked her out the door.

"Laura, your manners," Lianna chided gleefully as Laura dragged her toward the bright blue Dodge Shadow idling in the driveway. "I'm shocked! You didn't thank the doctor for his hospitality this weekend."

And from years of self-ingrained efforts toward perfection came Laura's reflexive polite words: "Thank you for—" She caught herself just in time. Breaking off in midsentence, Laura hustled a giggling Lianna into the car.

Jason watched them go. Although he knew he hadn't lied to kindly old Uncle George about Laura's whereabouts, he felt guilty anyway. And that sister of hers! Jason inhaled sharply. He wasn't a snob, he assured himself, but he sure wouldn't want a hooker as a sister-in-law.

Sister-in-law? Now where had that come from? He was thoroughly shaken by the renegade thought. If his mind was subconsciously heading down the matrimonial track, he was in far deeper than he'd ever dreamed. Than he'd ever wanted to be. A spasm of irrational panic seized him. He'd spent his entire adult life merrily skimming along the emotional surface; suddenly everything was different and he didn't understand. He wasn't ready to understand.

His immediate instinct was to withdraw and escape. He wanted his carefree, commitment-free life to continue just as it always had. And it would, he attempted to assure himself. If the Fletcher luck held—*and it had to!*—there would be no infant repercussions from this weekend and he would never have to see Laura Novak again. The Hospital Center was an enormous place. He could easily avoid her—and he would.

Could it get any worse than this? Laura wondered as she stared blindly through the windshield listening to Lianna prattle on.

"I can't believe it! I never thought I'd live to see the day! Laura, you spent a hot weekend with a man! And not merely a man—a hunk! With the body of a—"

"Lianna, please!" Laura interrupted, pleading. "I don't want to talk about it—ever! And you have to promise never to tell Uncle George and Aunt Sally about this."

Lianna gave her head an impatient shake. "Why not? You wanted the guy, he wanted you, and you both acted on it. Aunt Sal and Uncle George wouldn't condemn you, Laura. Why, they'd be thrilled to know that you're finally beginning to come alive. That you're human after all, with all the feelings and needs of a flesh-and-blood woman."

"You sound like a confessions magazine. Lianna, I made a terrible mistake. I—"

"Congratulations! At last I have a sister I can relate to. Do you know what an intimidating paragon of perfection you've always been? I used to wonder if you were a robot—like one of those creepy Stepford wives. Why, I've never even seen you sweat! At the end of a hot day when everyone else is looking wilted and rumpled and hot, in walks Laura, crisp and fresh and cool, not a hair out of place. Do you have any idea how demoralizing being around you can be?"

"I wish you wouldn't say things like that," Laura whispered, staring down at her hands.

"You didn't kiss the doctor good-bye," Lianna persisted. "You didn't even *say* good-bye. Why not? Did you have a fight or something? Is that why you called me to bring you home?"

Laura shrugged silently. When the silence extended for several long minutes, Lianna pressed on. "What went wrong, Laura? Did you tell him that you were madly in love with him? Knowing you, you thought you were if you went to bed with him. Men get scared when they hear the L-word, unless they say it first. And it definitely wouldn't go over with a smooth operator like Jason Fletcher. The man himself, his home, his car all scream elusive bachelor."

Laura said nothing. She wasn't about to dissect her weekend with Jason, not with Lianna or anyone else. The memories were too vivid, the hurt too intense.

"Okay, okay, I won't badger you anymore," Lianna finally said with a defeated sigh. "And if Uncle George and Aunt Sal ask, I'll say I picked you up at your friend Dana's place. But, Laura, if you ever feel the need to talk . . . Well, keep in mind I'm an expert at picking Mr. Wrongs. And I know how bad it feels when things don't work out the way you thought they would."

Laura winced. How could she tell Lianna that she hadn't thought at all beyond the sound of Jason's voice or the touch of his hand? Of his body moving over hers, their male and female strength fused together in a bond so strong and so pleasurable that she couldn't imagine never experiencing it again.

But she wouldn't. She'd observed Jason's indifference firsthand; she'd seen his cold gray eyes dismiss her. He was through with her. She'd be a bigger fool than she already was to presume otherwise. And now she must marshal up every ounce of her courage, strength, and pride to face him at the hospital every day and carry out her responsibilities without letting her personal problems affect her performance.

Her past successes bolstered her resolve. How many times had she been hurting inside, silently crying unshed tears while smoothly doing everything that was expected of her—and more? Why, almost all her life! And she would do it again, come tomorrow and all the tomorrows after that.

Six

Although the day shift at the Hospital Center didn't begin until seven, Laura made it a point to arrive fifteen minutes earlier to help the night staff with such final duties as checking the floor's narcotics stock and running through the daily prescription orders and renewals. Having worked night duty herself at Farview Memorial, she was aware of the nighttime personnel's desire to leave as close to their quitting time as possible.

Promptly at seven, the daylight nursing staff gathered to listen to the taped report of the patients' past eight hours in the small office off the nurses' station. Laura sipped her hot black coffee and made notes while following the report with the patient cardex. She'd already made the daily patient assignments to each nurse and nursing assistant and set up the teams and team leaders who in turn reported to her.

Listening to the taped patient report with the staff today were the three clinical nursing instructors from the three separate schools of nursing affiliated with the Hospital Center. Laura introduced herself to them as the others filed out to begin their patient care. She was slightly apprehensive about her role as liaison between the orthopedics floor and the schools. It was completely new to her; the last time she'd been around nursing instructors had been as a student nurse.

The Hospital Center was unusual in that it was affiliated with three separate nursing schools: a university with a four-year degree program, the Hospital Center's own three-year diploma school, and the community college's two-year associate degree program. All three qualified their students to take the state examination boards to become registered nurses.

Laura was aware of the controversy and infighting among nursing educators and hoped she wouldn't be caught in the middle of it here. As head nurse, it was her duty to screen and recommend patients to the three nursing instructors—Ms. St. Cyr from the AD program, Ms. Pecoraro of the Hospital Center's diploma school, and Ms. Long of the university's nursing school—and they in turn would assign their students to those patients.

"We're delighted to begin the new fall term with a new face here on orthopedics," Ms. Pecoraro greeted Laura warmly. "I'm sure we'll have a long and productive association, Ms. Novak."

Ms. Long was smiling too. "When I heard there was a new head nurse on ortho, I wanted to cheer. Frankly, I'd come to dread our rotation here. As you probably know, one of the most prominent and influential surgeons on this floor has a pathological aversion to all nursing students."

"A few years ago, there were a few—er—unfortunate mistakes involving some student nurses and from then on Dr. Fletcher absolutely refused to allow any of his patients to be assigned to any of our students," injected Ms. St. Cyr.

Laura swallowed. "Dr. Fletcher?" she asked carefully.

"He just returned from Ireland so you probably haven't met him yet," said Ms. Long. "We have great hopes that you'll be able to convince him to allow our students to work with his patients, Ms. Novak. Nancy Evans, the former head nurse here, backed Fletcher's boycott of our students so there was no support from her."

"But with Mrs. Evans gone and the new head nurse firmly behind us, we're hopeful that we can finally convince Dr. Fletcher to give our students another chance," Ms. Pecoraro said happily. "He's a gifted surgeon and his cases are always interesting. All the students would benefit from working with him and his patients."

Laura stared at the three expectant faces. They were pinning their hopes of winning Jason Fletcher's approval on *her*? If it weren't so awful, the situation would be downright funny.

She bid the three instructors good-bye with a false brave smile. Next week they would return to the floor with their students. Laura abruptly pushed the thought from her mind. There was enough to do right now without worrying about next week, she reminded herself firmly, and turned her attention to the daily patient census listing preops, transfers, and discharges.

When he wasn't scheduled for the operating room, Jason began his day with rounds on the Shock/Trauma Unit at seven before proceeding to the orthopedics floor. Though he'd been away for the past six weeks, he checked in with the Shock/Trauma staff anyway. He was seated in the spacious nursing station there when Casey Flynn strode in, dressed in his surgical scrub clothes. He flopped down onto the chair next to Jason and reached for a chart.

"You look like hell, Flynn," Jason remarked, glancing at him.

"I spent the last four hours in surgery with a ruptured abdominal aneurysm." Case gulped the coffee one of the nurses handed him. "The guy is only thirty-three years old and we almost lost him twice on the table."

Jason frowned. "Is he going to make it?"

Case crossed his fingers for luck. After a few more swallows of coffee, he focused again on Jason. "Hey, Fletch, where were you yesterday? We had a birthday cake for you and you never showed." He flashed a grin. "We ate the cake anyway."

Jason hit his forehead with the palm of his hand. "I'm sorry, Case, I forgot all about it. I—er—got tied up and—"

"Tied up, huh?" Case chuckled. "Let's see, was that Monique or Marcy who specialized in—"

"I wasn't with either of them," Jason interrupted and hastily added, "I wasn't with anyone. I was recovering from an acute case of jet lag. I slept straight through the weekend."

"Alone?" Case looked incredulous.

Jason shifted uncomfortably. "Yeah." He'd never lied to Case before. On the contrary, he usually boasted of his conquests! But Jason knew that no matter what, he was never going to tell Case or anyone else that Laura had spent the weekend with him. His attack of chivalry unnerved him. "So how was your Labor Day bash?" he asked, eager to divert the line of questioning from himself. "Did your nine thousand relatives and Sharla's nine million relatives all show up?"

Case nodded. "They were all there. But I only have three sisters, three nieces, and three nephews, Fletch. A trifle short of nine thousand. And Sharla—" He broke off with a laugh. "Yeah, there *are* nine million Shakarians, all right."

"And they're all connected with the Hospital Center in some way or another." Jason rose to leave. "Well, I'd better head down to ortho. There's no use putting it off any longer." He heaved a sigh.

"I can't believe Nancy Evans won't be there. She was one of the finest nurses I've ever worked with. I was only half kidding when I told her to try to talk her husband out of taking his promotion and transfer so she could stay here."

Case murmured a consoling remark and continued to write on the chart.

Jason gave his friend a friendly thump on the shoulder and strode off. On Six-West, the orthopedics floor, he gathered a group of residents, interns, and medical students together in preparation for the rounds of his patients' rooms at eight o'clock. He spotted Zane Montrose in the group and nodded to him. Was Montrose going to continue his pursuit of Laura? The question sprang involuntarily to mind. Jason wasn't pleased with the punched-in-the-gut feeling that accompanied it.

"Where's the new head nurse?" he asked, checking his watch. The head nurse always accompanied the doctors on their rounds, making and taking notes. "It's already three minutes after eight." Jason frowned. "Nancy was never late."

At that moment, the three nursing instructors left the nurses' station, talking among themselves. "They're b-a-a-a-ck," Stan Gloz, Chief Resident, familiar with Jason's ongoing feud with the nursing schools, chanted in a singsong voice.

Jason opened his mouth to toss off a wisecrack of his own, but the words were wiped from his mind the moment he saw Laura enter the nurses' station from the adjacent office. She looked like a picture-book nurse, dressed in a starched white uniform with pleated front, skirt hemmed to the middle of her knee. She wore the required white hose and white espadrille-style nurses' shoes. Her nursing school pin and cap were properly affixed, and her hair was neatly tied back with a thin white satin ribbon. She looked flawless, impeccably professional. And somewhat of a nursing throwback. These days most nurses wore two-piece slacks-and-top uniforms with white running shoes. The caps, once a symbol, were seldom worn anymore.

What was she doing here? The question barely had a chance to register in his brain when Laura joined the group. She smiled at them collectively, the quintessential cool, calm, competent professional. Light years removed from the passionate, intensely responsive woman he had held in his arms.

"I'm sorry I'm a few minutes late," Laura said smoothly. "I'm ready to begin whenever you are, Dr. Fletcher."

Jason stared down at the clipboard and pen she was holding. His eyes lifted to her name pin, attached to her uniform slightly above her breast. LAURA NOVAK, RN. HEAD NURSE, it read. "You're not—" he began hoarsely. "You can't be—"

"I'm the new head nurse here on orthopedics," Laura injected in those same serene, dulcet tones. Years of practice kept her outwardly steady while she suppressed her raging inner feelings. Seeing Jason had an actual physical impact on her. Her stomach was lurching and her heart was pounding. She wanted to scream at him for using her and then coldly withdrawing his loving warmth. She wanted to burst into tears and sob out the hurt she'd been suffering since she'd left his house. She wanted to throw her arms around him and beg him to hold her. All at the same time.

But the medical group assembled in the corridor saw only a composed, meticulous woman with a somewhat reserved smile and fathomless blue-gray-green eyes.

They'd spent the weekend in bed together and she hadn't mentioned that they would be working together, that they would see each other every weekday here in the hospital? Jason was shaken to his very core. And not hiding it as well as Laura was. "They replaced Nancy with *you*?" he demanded sharply and the group eyed Laura with a mixture of speculation and apprehension.

She never batted an eye; her expression never changed.

Her imperturbable facade only increased Jason's ire. But he was quite aware of the others, staring from him to Laura. His outburst must seem incomprehensible to them, and he quickly sought to rectify the situation.

"Nancy Evans was at least ten years older than you are!" he exclaimed, seeking a plausible reason for his protests and using the first that sprang to mind. "You're way too young to be able to handle all the responsibilities of the head nurse position."

"Hey, Jason, give the kid a chance," the chief resident interjected. "She used to work as night shift charge nurse in orthopedics in a community hospital. She knows the ropes."

"Thank you, Stan," said Laura. "I appreciate the vote of confidence." She'd never doubted her abilities as a nurse, but Jason's skepticism hurt.

"Ortho in a community hospital consists of kids with minor broken bones and routine disk surgery. Anything more complex is sent here," Jason replied. "And what about scheduling? The head nurse has to make up the nurses' and aides' schedules covering all three shifts seven days a week, taking into account days off, holidays, vacations, and shift rotations. It used to drive Nancy crazy!"

"I had no idea you were so concerned with nursing scheduling," joked Stan. "Laura, if you need any help making out the schedules, just ask Dr. Fletcher here."

Laura smiled sweetly, smoothly, giving nothing away.

None of the younger members of the group dared to say anything. Jason abruptly saw himself in their eyes: a raging prima donna hurtling toward midlife and resenting the youth behind him. He was appalled. It isn't like that, he wanted to tell them. He glared at Laura, fury burning in his eyes. If she'd leveled with him, he could have prepared himself for this meeting, but she had preferred to let him find out this way.

Tight-lipped, he turned away from her. "Let's go," he said brusquely and led the group to the end of the hall.

The chief resident took charge, filling Jason in on the newest patients, quizzing the medical students about their condition and progress. Laura walked slightly apart from them, concentrating on her notes and carefully keeping her distance from Jason.

A few of Jason's patients who had been admitted before he'd left for his sabbatical were still there. One was young Terry Trice, a seventeen-year-old high school football star who'd broken his neck in a scrimmage at a summer training camp. Tragically, his spinal cord had been severed and the boy was paralyzed from the chest down.

The group gathered near his room to discuss the case in hushed voices.

"Terry has been increasingly depressed and moody," reported Zane Montrose, who was assigned to the patient. "He feels lonely and isolated. His family is here every day, of course, but his friends' visits have dropped off. I guess you can expect that from high school kids but—"

"No," Jason cut in sharply. "I don't think we should expect that from high school kids. I think we should expect them to care about a kid who was playing for the school team and ended up permanently disabled. I think we should make damn sure that they get their asses in here and make every effort to keep Terry's spirits up. They're healthy, they're whole, and that's the least they can do. Nancy, make a note that I'm to call the principal of that high school and make arrangements to speak at a special assembly. I'm going to make damn sure that every teacher and kid in that school feels a responsibility to come visit Terry."

"Hey, that's a great idea, Jason." Stan Gloz beamed his approval. "When Fletcher gets fired up, there's nobody who'll say no to him. Terry Trice will have plenty of company after you've laid it on the line at his school. Oh, and Fletch, for future reference, our head nurse's name is Laura. Nancy is in Seattle these days, remember?"

"Don't remind me," muttered Jason, stepping into Terry Trice's room.

Laura felt hot color flood her cheeks. While Jason had been talking about young Terry, she'd forgotten the acrimony between them. She admired his concern for his patient, his determination to help the boy and his willingness to go beyond the orthopedic call of duty to do it. But Jason hadn't forgotten that he wanted no part of her! The acknowledgment hurt. And not only did he consider her easy, he also doubted her nursing skills. She felt like crying.

And tears did fill her eyes when she observed Jason with Terry Trice in the corner room filled with Mylar balloons, sports pennants, pictures, posters, and get-well cards. Jason was so good with Terry, so natural. He teased him, he discussed sports with him, he'd even brought him a souvenir from his trip to Belfast—an autographed photo of the champion Irish soccer team and a soccer jersey.

Laura remembered how kind Jason had been when she was hysterical with the suppressed grief and fear from her parents' accident. And she thought of those wonderful, tender, passionate hours in bed with him and knew in that instant that he was the man she could love and respect and admire for the rest of her life.

But he despised her. She just knew it.

After rounds were completed, the group scattered. Laura sat down at the desk to transcribe the verbal orders to the charts where they would be co-signed by the doctors later. She was reaching for the first chart when a hand closed around her upper arm.

Jason's voice growled against her ear. "I want to speak to you."

Laura rose shakily to her feet, desperately fighting for control. If only he would remove his hand, if only he would hold onto her forever. . . . Her brain seemed to be rioting. She had never felt such conflict in her life.

They entered the small office adjacent to the nurses' station and Jason purposefully closed the door behind them. Laura's eyes widened when she saw him press in the doorknob lock.

But when he dropped his hand from her arm and she turned to face him, she was as cool and calm and collected as a head nurse meeting with a physician should be. She might be dying inside, but she had too much pride to ever let him know.

"Why didn't you tell me you were the new head nurse here on Six-West?" Jason demanded without any opening preliminaries. "What kind of game are you playing, lady?"

"I'm not playing games." Laura took a step backward. "I—I didn't deliberately try to keep it from you, Jason. The few times I tried to tell you at the picnic, you interrupted me and then later . . ." She lowered her eyes and swallowed. "The subject didn't come up."

"The subject didn't come up!" he echoed with a ferocious scowl. "Whose fault is that, Miss Novak? You knew who I was. Didn't it occur to you that working together after—*after*!—was going to be damn difficult, if not impossible?"

She stared down at her impeccably polished white shoes. "Not until Monday morning," she whispered.

"Ah, yes, the classic morning-after reckoning." His voice was cruel. "You could have at least forewarned me then that I would be meeting you again here on the floor as the prim and proper Miss Novak, Head Nurse."

"How could I?" Her voice rose and her jewel-toned eyes flashed. "I was too mortified with myself for spending a weekend indulging in—in cheap sex with a veritable stranger!"

For some reason, her abrupt loss of composure disturbed him almost as much as it distressed her. He stared at her quivering mouth, watched her restless hand motions. "It wasn't cheap sex, Laura," he murmured deeply, his eyes holding hers. "It was great sex. Believe me, I know the difference."

She took a deep breath. "I—I was sure that you thought I was nothing but an—an easy score."

"No!" He unconsciously took a step nearer. "Never that, Laura."

A tiny spark of hope lit her heart. She gazed at him, her beautiful eyes wistful and earnest. "I was positive that you never intended to see me again."

"You were right on target there." Jason gave his head a wry shake. He didn't believe in lying; it was unfair, not good sportsmanship. "That's partly why learning that you were working here was such a shock."

Odd, how things had worked out, he thought with a calm that surprised him: she might be pregnant and they would be working together daily. Their coming together began to seem like it was fated, if you believed in such things, which Jason never had . . . until, perhaps, right now.

The hopeful spark kindling in Laura was extinguished under a crush of pain. Humiliation and self-anger washed over her in waves. How could she be so stupid and romantically naive to think, even for a moment, that he cared for her? The message he was giving her was the same one she'd already figured out. He'd simply prettied up the words. *He hadn't planned on seeing her again.*

It hurt so much, but she wasn't about to make things worse by letting him see how deeply he had wounded her. She cast around frantically in her brain for just the right comeback. What would her sister do in a situation like this, she wondered wildly. Lianna's romantic past bordered on the catastrophic; she had a frightening talent for finding exactly the type of man who was all wrong for her. A confrontation like this would be nothing new for Lianna. She would make some sardonic joke or wisecrack.

Laura had her answer. She would play it Lianna's way. Straightening her shoulders, locking her renegade emotions away, she raised her brows and said lightly, "Great sex, cheap sex, whatever you want to call it, it obviously wasn't an experience you found worth repeating, since you planned to avoid me for the rest of your life." She even managed a sickly smile.

"Laura, it's not like that!" Jason began to perspire. Damn, he was making a mess of it! He felt like a world-class heel. But how could he tell her that he had to keep his distance from her because she was the first woman he wanted to keep close? He wondered if he were becoming unhinged.

"Oh, it's exactly like that," Laura said blithely. Once in character, she possessed the inner strength to carry out the charade. "So let's agree to forget the weekend ever happened. I'm sure we're both mature enough and sophisticated enough to work together without allowing any negative personal feelings to interfere with our professional roles."

Perversely, her cool dismissal of everything they had shared irritated him immensely, when it should have brought a sigh of relief. Maybe he was already unhinged, Jason decided grimly.

"If you'll excuse me, I have a million things to do this morning." Her automatic smile was friendly but detached. She was the personification of nursely cool, of professional politeness. Laura walked past him to the door and unlocked it.

"It's not that easy, Laura."

The ominous note in his voice froze her in her tracks. She turned around to face him. "W-What do you mean?"

He was pleased he'd broken through her maddening aplomb, not bothering to wonder why it was so important that she be open and vulnerable to him. "I mean that I didn't protect you—us—as well as I should have this past weekend," he said gruffly. "Laura, if you're pregnant, I want to—"

Laura didn't hear another thing. *Pregnant!* Her mind went hurtling into the stratospheres of shock. She'd never given that possibility a thought! This was a nurse? She scorned herself. She did some swift and silent counting. "I'm not pregnant. I—I can't be!" she cried, drawing in huge gulps of air. "It's—the wrong time of the month."

Jason arched his brows. "I wonder how many people are walking around today whose mothers once uttered those exact words?"

"No, really. My—My p-period is due tomorrow."

"Tomorrow?"

She nodded vigorously. Odd, she should be mortified having this conversation with Jason, but she wasn't. Perhaps she'd already passed her mortification point. Or perhaps she and Jason had already shared so much intimacy that such discussions were perfectly natural between them. She twisted her lips into a forced smile. "So you see, you have nothing to worry about. Now, I really must—"

"Maybe the biology courses in reproduction we had in medical school were more detailed than the ones taught in the nursing schools. We learned that timing could be an extremely unreliable factor in fertility. We do have something to worry about, Laura. And I want you to promise to tell me the truth. You can trust me to do the right thing."

"I'll tell you the moment you're—we're safe, I promise. And we will be," she added and then fled the office. She didn't even want to know what he considered the right thing. Paying for a speedy abortion? Or forcing himself to go through a meaningless wedding ceremony with his eye on a speedy divorce? Either option chilled her.

"Laura, Mrs. Madison in six-fourteen wants to talk to you about hiring a private duty nurse for her husband after his hip surgery tomorrow." One of the younger nurses caught Laura as she headed for the pile of charts. "Do you have time to talk to her now?"

"Of course." Laura was delighted to escape to room 614 and talk to Mrs. Madison. It was a relief to focus her thoughts on a patient's problems rather than her own. It had long been her way of coping.

After her discussion with Mrs. Madison, she paid a brief visit to every patient to check on them and register any problems or complaints they might have, something she did at least once a day. Much of the head nurse's work was administrative and she missed the actual patient care she'd given at Farview Memorial. At least her own daily rounds provided her with some patient contact.

She was calm and composed as she reentered the nurses' station a half hour later. When Zane Montrose approached her, she stifled a groan and summoned up her best friendly-yet-remote head nurse smile. They discussed his patients for a while and then Zane cleared his throat and said urgently, "Laura, I'd like to talk to you about something personal."

She braced herself for him to ask her out. He did it every other day, and she refused just as regularly.

"Laura, I've never apologized for what happened your first day here when I, uh, came on to you on the way to the cafeteria." His face flooded with color. "It was stupid and crude and—well, I'm sorry."

She stared impassively. "I accept your apology." Her voice was cool.

Zane gulped. "I know I blew any chance I might have had with you . . ." He paused, as if waiting for her to deny it. She didn't and he sighed and continued, "I don't usually act that way, you know. No, I guess you don't know. I was showing off, acting like a big shot. You see, Stan Gloz had been kidding me, saying that I'd never get anywhere with you and I wanted to show him that I could." He shrugged sheepishly. "I guess I proved him right instead."

"Zane, let's just forget it and put it behind us. I'm sure we're both mature enough to work together without allowing any personal feelings to interfere with our professional roles." She should tape that particular little speech, Laura thought wryly, it was the second time she'd used it this morning.

"Can we start over as friends?" Zane persisted.

Laura smiled. "Of course." She waited for him to ask her out; she intended to refuse, of course.

But he merely flashed a relieved smile. "I'm glad, Laura."

Their hushed little conference in the corner of the nurses' station did not go unobserved. Standing in the corridor nearby, Jason Fletcher had been discussing the next day's surgery schedule with the chief resident when he'd seen Zane Montrose approach Laura. He watched them as they talked, as they exchanged smiles.

When Stan Gloz repeated his question for the third time, he became aware that Jason's attention was elsewhere and followed his line of vision. Stan chuckled. "You have to give Montrose credit for persistence. Laura Novak doesn't have the time of day for him, but he doesn't give up. I knew he didn't stand a chance with her from the moment they met. She looked *through* him, not at him."

Jason scowled. "Yeah, well, she's looking at him now." The sight of Laura smiling at Zane Montrose burned him like acid. "Excuse me, Stan, I, uh, forgot to chart an order."

He strode away from the bemused doctor, forgetting that he wasn't possessive about the women in his life, that he'd never suffered a single pang of sexual jealousy over anyone. He swept into the station and hooked an arm around Laura's waist. "I just remembered something I forgot to mention when we were talking earlier," he said, literally turning her away from Zane Montrose. He sent the younger man an unmistakable dismissive glance.

Reluctantly, Zane moved away.

"What did you want to say?" Laura demanded and was dismayed by the breathless catch in her voice. It was difficult to keep calm and unruffled when he was looking at her with those fiery gray eyes. She tried to unobtrusively disengage herself from Jason's hold.

He tightened his fingers over her hip in a frankly sexually possessive way. "Keep away from Montrose," he said through clenched teeth. "I'm not going to stand by and watch you tumble into his arms on the rebound."

"Oh!" Fury ripped through her and a fine red haze seemed to appear in front of her eyes. She'd heard the expression "seeing red"; truly she was doing exactly that. "On the rebound from what?" Laura could not remember ever being so angry in her entire life. Her face was flushed and her body was trembling with the force of it. "From a cheap weekend fling with a man who admitted he never wanted to see me again?"

She jerked herself away from him so fiercely that she stumbled backward and went barreling into an interested medical student who was trying hard to pretend he wasn't eavesdropping avidly.

Jason started toward her. The wide-eyed medical student jumped out of his way. "Come into the office." His voice was low, intense, authoritative. "I want to talk to you alone. Right now!" Few, if any, of his co-workers would have refused to cooperate when he used that tone.

Laura did. "No!"

"No?" He was astounded by her refusal. "I gave you an order, *Miss Novak.*" A fresh wave of anger flooded him. "You'll damn well do as I say."

For years she had been a model of nursely decorum, ever the tactful diplomat when dealing with a temperamental physician. Not this time. "Don't think you can bully me by pulling rank, *Dr. Fletcher.*" Her eyes snapped with anger. "You have nothing to say to me that is worth hearing!"

Jason stared at her, nonplussed. He'd never been in this situation. It wasn't that he hadn't heard the word "no" from a woman before. But when he did, it was generally an amused, fond rebuff in response to his light pass, never a furious refusal. And he'd never heard it on the job, from nurse to physician. Laura's defiance was a first. But then, they weren't in their doctor-nurse roles now, were they?

"This is what happens when you get involved with someone you work with," he muttered, more to himself than to her. "This is why I've always kept away from any nurse on orthopedics or Shock/ Trauma. But you—"

"Yes, it's all my fault. I concealed my true identity, I deceived you, and I seduced you." Laura was somewhere beyond rage. None of her colleagues at Farview Memorial would've recognized this flushed, flashing-eyed spitfire as the perfect, placid Miss Novak. "Why don't you report me to the director of nursing for insubordination and sexual harassment? I'm sure you have the makings of a landmark case!"

She stormed off, leaving him slack-jawed, staring after her.

Audrey, one of the part-time nurses, apprehended her as she reached the chart rack. "Laura, Mrs. Kessler in six-oh-one is complaining of severe pain. She had back surgery yesterday and I gave her an injection of Dilaudid less than an hour ago which should've helped." The nurse frowned. "Unless something's happened that caused her pain to increase. I told Dr. Montrose, but he dismissed the possibility that anything might be wrong. He thinks Mrs. K. is making a bid for attention."

Laura gave her head a shake to clear it. It wasn't easy to swing from a highly emotional state into cool professionalism. She'd never had the problem before; now, thanks to Jason Fletcher, she was experiencing it for the first time. She shot a baleful glance in his direction. To her consternation, he was watching her and glowered back.

Laura swiftly turned her complete attention to the other nurse. "I'll go talk to Mrs. Kessler, Audrey. And I'll ask Dr. Montrose to check her too, just in case."

"That guy really gets on my nerves," Audrey said sourly. "'He has a severe attitude problem. He doesn't take seriously anything a nurse tells him about a patient."

Zane Montrose was going to listen to her and check out Mrs. Kessler, Laura decided grimly, no matter how charming she had to be to get him to do it. Determined and focused, she walked over to Zane to discuss Mrs. Kessler, not glancing at Jason who hadn't taken his eyes off her.

When he saw Laura approach Zane Montrose, Jason was certain that his blood pressure reading would shoot off the gauge. She was deliberately trying to provoke him, he raged inwardly. She was trying to drive him crazy. Worse, she was succeeding. He was so preoccupied with the infuriating scene of Laura and Zane talking and smiling that he didn't notice the chief resident amble up to him.

"So that's the way it is, huh? Montrose isn't the only one with eyes for our Miss Novak." Stan looked amused. "My wife and I saw you with her at the picnic, but we would never have guessed there was anything between you two. She doesn't seem like your type."

"She's not my type. And there's nothing between us."

"Sure. You always jump over the desk to tear the head nurse away from a first-year resident. I saw that hot little fight between you two, Fletch. Everybody else did too."

"It was simply a professional disagreement," Jason insisted. Why didn't he just tell Stan that he'd laid Miss Novak after the picnic so they could share a comradely, macho laugh? Gloomily, he rejected the notion out of hand. As much as he didn't want to, he felt protective of her. And possessive. What had happened between them was too private and too intimate to share with anyone. It meant too much to joke about.

He and Stan watched Laura and Zane walk down the hall together toward the patient rooms. Stan's gaze darted from the retreating couple to Jason's bleak countenance. "Whoa, Fletch, you've got it bad and that ain't good," he paraphrased the old blues lyrics.

"Put a lid on it, Stan."

Jason rallied himself. Stan had it all wrong; he didn't care about Laura Novak, he assured himself. The moment she got her period and he was totally in the clear, he would never give her another thought. He would be having too much fun. In fact, it was about time that he resumed his social life. He'd been out of touch since his six-week sojourn abroad. Who should he call first? he wondered with a predatory smile. Elena? Caryn? Or maybe he should start at the beginning of the alphabet with Abbi.

Seven

Restlessly, Jason paced through his house that evening, going from one empty room to another. It was the first time he'd ever remembered feeling lonely in it. Memories of his weekend with Laura assailed him at every turn. He wanted her, he missed her. Reluctantly, he admitted to himself that no other woman's presence would suffice. His leather address book filled with phone numbers lay untouched beside the bedside telephone.

He stood in the hallway and stared into his bedroom, remembering Laura in it, wishing she were there now. Abruptly, he walked toward the second bedroom which he had converted into a super video-audio center with all the latest equipment. None of it interested him at the moment and he continued his walk down the hall to the third bedroom, which served as a guest room. It was decorated functionally and uninterestingly, but was a fairly large room. It could easily be converted into a nursery, if the need should arise.

Oddly enough, this time the thought didn't give him palpitations. After all, it was only one room, he reasoned; everything else in the house wouldn't have to be displaced. All the baby paraphernalia would fit in here with no trouble at all.

And it wasn't as if he were a poor, struggling medical student who would have to moonlight for extra cash to support a child while studying and paying tuition. His current investments were already enough to guarantee all the necessities and luxuries of child-rearing right up to and including college.

He liked the idea of providing for his little family; he thought of his own parents who had delighted in giving him whatever he wanted. They would go bonkers over a grandchild! They never pushed or pressured him to produce one, of course, but he remembered his birthday call from them yesterday. His mother had talked a lot about how cute and lovable their neighbors' visiting grandchildren were. It went without saying that her own—Jason's children—would be the cutest and most lovable of them all.

Impulsively, Jason reached for the phone.

The phone rang for the tenth time in the past thirty minutes.

"Laura, will you answer it?" Lianna was pacing the wood-paneled family room like a caged tiger.

Laura looked up from the historical romance she was attempting to read. "You know it's Ted, Lianna," she said mildly. "He's been calling on an average of every three minutes. Why don't you answer it so you can hang up on him again?"

"Because he doesn't seem to be getting the message!" Lianna said firmly. "I don't want to talk to him, I want him to quit calling me. You tell him, Laura. Use your sternest, most repressive nurse voice. Maybe then he'll believe it."

"Why don't we just let it ring?" suggested Laura. "Maybe Ted will think you've gone out and hang up on his own. And maybe he'll stop calling," she added hopefully.

"He won't. And that infernal ringing is driving me nuts! *Please,* Laura!"

Sighing, Laura laid her book down and went into the kitchen to pick up the phone. She hated getting embroiled in Lianna's romantic messes; still, it might be worth it this time if she could convince the tenacious Ted to stop calling. The incessant ringing and subsequent phone-slamming that had gone on this evening was becoming very annoying.

"Hello?" She hoped she sounded sufficiently forbidding.

"I was beginning to think no one was there."

Laura came close to letting the receiver slip from her fingers. It wasn't the hapless Ted on the end of the line. It was Jason Fletcher. She took a full moment to recover from the shock. And then her heart went into overdrive, slamming wildly against her rib cage. "I'm here," she finally managed lamely.

"I've been thinking about the weekend," came Jason's deep, low voice.

He sounded sexy, bringing back memories of that voice soft in her ear, as he reached for her in the darkness of the night. Laura shivered. And instantly regained control of herself. He was probably thinking about the weekend with horror and regret, blaming her for deceiving him and trying to trap him.

"Laura, I've been wondering if—"

"I know exactly what you're wondering," she interrupted icily. "And you have nothing to worry about no matter what happens!"

Laura slammed the receiver into its cradle and stalked back into the living room. The phone began to ring the moment she stepped over the threshold.

Lianna groaned. "Ted didn't believe you? What do I have to do to get through to that guy? Maybe I could threaten to arrest him for—for harassment by telephone." She frowned, considering. "Of course I'm not sure if there is such a charge, not when there haven't been any threats or obscenities, but I'll give it a try." She rushed to answer the phone. "Laura, it's for you," she called a moment later.

"Find out who it is and say I'll call back later."

Before Laura could exhale, Lianna was at her side. "Laura, it's Jason Fletcher. He says it's very important that he talk to you immediately."

"No." Laura shook her head. "I don't want to talk to him."

"Laura, for heaven's sake, the man is gorgeous. He's a doctor. He's rich. You spent the weekend with him, Laura. Of course you want to talk to him!"

Laura picked up her book and went upstairs to her room without another word. *Don't think,* she cautioned herself. *Don't feel. Just be thankful that this is Uncle George and Aunt Sally's bowling night and they're not here to witness this fiasco.* She lay across her bed on her stomach and forced herself to concentrate on the printed pages before her.

A moment later, the phone began to ring again. "I can't take this!" Lianna wailed from the foot of the stairs. "Now we don't know if it's Ted or Jason Fletcher calling. I'm going out to get away from the damn phone. Want to come with me, Laura?"

Laura hopped to her feet, abandoning her book without a second thought. "I'll drive," she said, reaching for her car keys.

Jason spent the morning in the operating room performing arthroscopic surgery on the knee of a defensive tackle for the University of Maryland. The procedure was successful and the patient was taken to the recovery room where he would be monitored until being sent to the orthopedics floor later in the day.

Jason was headed to the cafeteria for lunch with a group of the operating room staff when he spotted Laura and three of the nurses from Six-West leaving the cafeteria.

His eyes swept over Laura. She was wearing her hair loose today, in a neatly smooth page-boy style, and her white uniform, cap, and shoes were as meticulously spotless as yesterday. His natural inclination was to go to her. Then he remembered how she'd hung up on him last night, how she'd told her sister that she didn't want to talk to him, and finally refused to answer the phone at all. His lips tightened into a straight line and he kept on walking.

"Aarrgh! The director of nursing!" gasped one of the OR nurses in the group. "And me looking like a bag lady. Quick! Hide me!" She slipped between two interns and a second-year resident.

"No sweat. She's not looking your way," one of the interns pointed out. "She's cornered a bunch of nurses leaving the cafeteria."

Jason looked ahead to see Clare Maridian, Director of Nursing, stop to talk to Laura and her group. An unholy smile lit his face. "You guys go on in without me. I think I'll wreak a little havoc among the director and her nurses."

He joined the nurses, slipping a friendly arm around Clare Maridian's shoulders. "Clare! You're looking fabulous as usual. Let me put in a good word for our terrific nurses on Six-West. I want you to make sure all of them get raises."

It took every bit of Laura's formidable control not to react to the sight of Jason and the director of nursing with their arms around each other, grinning like longtime pals. *Or former lovers?* Her eyes widened. Clare Maridian was slim, pretty, and in her midforties, light years removed from the bulky, stone-faced and close-to-seventy-year-old battle-ax who served as director of nursing at Farview Memorial.

It wasn't inconceivable that Jason Fletcher and Clare Maridian might've had an affair; the scope of Jason's amours was hospital legend. Watching them together made it seem quite conceivable indeed. Jealousy shot through Laura like a poisoned dart and was quickly compounded by a flash of horror. Just yesterday she'd challenged Jason: ". . . *Report me to the director of nursing for insubordination and sexual harassment.*" Laura repressed the urge to groan aloud.

"Clare, what's this I hear about your cute little cousin Dana and ortho's own Zane Montrose?" Jason continued jovially, shooting a quick glance at Laura.

Clara laughed. "Don't tell me it's all over the hospital already! Then you probably know Dana went out with him Saturday after the picnic and Sunday and Monday nights too."

Jason looked pleased. "Hey, that's great! I know I'm hoping the two of them will live happily ever after. How about you, Miss Novak?"

He had the supreme satisfaction of catching her totally off guard. Laura blushed and stammered a few obligatory good wishes. She glanced quickly at her watch. "We'd better get back to the floor," she said to her three companions.

"I was hoping that you'd have time for a quick update on what we were discussing yesterday, Miss Novak," Jason inserted smoothly. "Since I've been in the OR all morning, I didn't have a chance to see you on the floor, and I'm going to my office right after lunch and seeing patients for the rest of the day. This is the only time we can talk."

"Take all the time you need, Laura," interjected one of the nurses. "We'll take care of business till you're back on the floor."

Clare Maridian nodded her approval.

Laura saw the triumph gleaming in Jason's mocking gray eyes. And some impulsive, devilish streak which she never dreamed she possessed sprang swiftly to the fore. "You've changed your mind about the nursing students!" she said with a bright, ingenuous smile, as if that was the subject they'd discussed yesterday. "You've reconsidered and are going to allow them to be assigned to your patients."

"Oh, Jason, how wonderful!" Clare Maridian exclaimed joyfully. "You don't know how much I was dreading your yearly feud with the nursing instructors." She gave Laura a look of real respect. "Miss Novak, I'm delighted you've been a successful intermediary."

Laura's gaze met Jason's. A few words from him—in front of the other nurses and the director herself—and her credibility and reputation would be wiped out. Jason knew it. And couldn't bring himself to say anything.

"Miss Novak, why not have a cup of coffee and iron out the details concerning the students while Jason eats lunch?" Clare suggested forcefully. She was all smiles, yet all business too. "After all, the students arrive on the floors next week." She bid Jason and Laura good-bye and hurried off, the other nurses following in her wake.

Laura and Jason were left standing alone in the corridor. An awkwardly tense silence descended over them. Jason was the first to break it. "Nice try, but it ain't gonna work, baby. I'm not letting those idiots near any of my patients."

Laura's temper, always so tightly reined, broke from its leash of restraint. "Nursing students are not idiots! You wouldn't dream of banning medical students from taking care of your patients. I can't believe you've been allowed to get away with it where student nurses are concerned."

"I'll tell you why I've been allowed to get away with it, honey. A few years ago, two nursing students were assigned to one of my patients who was in a Stryker frame. They forgot to strap him in when they turned him and he fell on the floor on his face. He wasn't badly hurt, thank God, but the family sued me for negligence and physical and emotional pain and suffering. They collected one point three million dollars. You might be aware that malpractice insurance rates for orthopedic surgeons are among the highest. Well, after that little incident, mine went even higher. And I'd done nothing except to cooperate with those schools!"

"That wasn't fair," Laura said softly. "You weren't to blame, the accident wasn't your fault. But it's not fair for you to hold every single nursing student responsible, either."

"Yes, well, sometimes life isn't fair, Laura." He started into the cafeteria. "You know that better than anyone. After what you've been through—"

"I don't want to talk about my past," Laura interrupted, automatically following him to the food line.

"Then let's talk about your future," he shot back. "And whether or not a little Fletcher is going to be in it."

Laura flushed scarlet. When she would have turned and rushed off, he caught her hand, chaining her to the spot. "You're not going anywhere, Laura. Your boss ordered you to have a cup of coffee and sit with me while I eat lunch. That's what you're going to do."

He held onto her hand until they reached the trays and utensils. Tense and silent, Laura followed him because she had no choice, wondering how many people saw his hand clasping hers.

"Do you want anything to eat?" he asked as he piled a plate of meat loaf, mashed potatoes, and brussels sprouts, a rather wilted green salad, and a piece of glutinous cherry pie on his tray.

"No, thank you." Laura shook her head. He was actually going to eat that stuff? The cafeteria wasn't noted for its cooking; cold sandwiches were the least lethal items on the menu. "I've already had lunch."

"I'm assuming nothing has happened to eliminate the possibility that you're pregnant?" he asked, getting a cup of coffee from the dispenser.

"I told you I'd let you know," Laura said rather desperately, glancing around. Fortunately no one was in hearing distance. "Just don't keep asking!"

Jason reached for a carton of milk. "I'm getting you this instead of coffee. Milk is more nutritional for a developing fetus," he added knowledgeably. "Besides, I've heard coffee can cause morning sickness."

"It's not morning, it's one o'clock in the afternoon. I want coffee, not milk, and there is no developing fetus!"

"We don't know that for sure, Laura." Jason paid for the food and selected an empty table in the almost empty cafeteria. He placed the milk and a straw in front of Laura. "Were you surprised to hear that Dana Shakarian and Zane Montrose hit it off so well at the picnic that they dated for the rest of the weekend?" he asked smoothly, stabbing his meat loaf with a fork.

"I was surprised to hear that Dana is Clare Maridian's cousin." Laura stared at the thick slice of meat loaf, smothered in congealing brown gravy, and shuddered.

"They're first cousins. I've lost track of how many members of the Shakarian family are affiliated with the Hospital Center, but there are quite a few of them." Jason gave her a bland smile. "I thought you ought to know about Dana's close relationship to your top boss before you tried to charm Zane Montrose away from her."

"I am not trying to charm Zane Montrose away from anyone!"

"I saw you flashing those come-hither smiles at him yesterday, honey. If you weren't trying to dazzle him, what were you trying to do? Make me jealous?"

Laura didn't know which point to refute first. So she went on the offensive instead. "What about you and *Clare?* I haven't seen such a sickening display of goo-goo eyes and flirty smiles since—since—"

"You were jealous!" Jason crowed, obviously delighted at the notion. He reached across the table and patted her hand with his. "Let me set the record straight, sweetie. Clare and I are buddies. I made a friendly pass at her when she first came to the hospital a few years ago and she very charmingly told me that she'd been married for twenty years, was the mother of two teenagers, and that I'd given her a good laugh and a healthy boost to her ego. We've been pals ever since."

"Oh, goody," Laura muttered under her breath.

Jason shifted slightly, moving his legs to either side of hers and then closing them to clasp her legs between his. Laura felt the muscular strength of his calves, warm against her legs, and her pulses jumped. His hold was unmistakably possessive; paradoxically, she felt both protected and captured. And consumed by sexual awareness of Jason Fletcher. Her body throbbed in rhythm with her heartbeat.

"Why wouldn't you talk to me last night when I called, Laura?" Jason asked, changing the subject so abruptly that Laura, her senses reeling from his potent grip, was caught without a ready answer.

"I didn't want to talk to you," was all she could come up with.

"I was concerned about you, Laura. I feel . . . a responsibility toward you." He knew it was the wrong thing to say the moment he said it. Storm clouds gathered in Laura's eyes.

"There's no reason for you to feel anything toward me," she said hotly, pulling her legs free from his and pushing back her chair. "I can do very well without your misguided sympathy or your misplaced sense of responsibility. *If* I'm pregnant I'll manage very well on my own."

"If you're pregnant, you won't have to manage on your own. I intend to marry you, of course.'

"Marry me?" Laura gaped at him.

Her astonishment irritated him. "Of course. What did you expect me to do? Write you a check and tell you to take care of the matter on your own?"

"I didn't know what to think. You said you never intended to see me again." She squelched the pain his bald admission still caused. "And thanks anyway but I'll pass on your commendable, but less than inviting, offer."

"Less than inviting?" Jason frowned. "Believe me, baby, there are a lot of women who would love to be Mrs. Jason Fletcher."

"Well, I'm not one of those countless thousands." She gave him an acidly sweet smile. "I'm not going to marry a man who feels it's his duty and his *responsibility* to marry me. Anyway, the point is moot. In a very short while we'll have positive proof that I'm not pregnant."

"And if we don't? You obviously haven't considered the situation very carefully, Laura." He visualized Laura's body growing round and full with his child and the image aroused rather than terrorized him. He thought about his plans to convert his unused room to a nursery for a new little Fletcher. "As I have," he added huskily.

"The situation is completely hypothetical, but *if* it were to happen, I'd go to New York City where I could get a job in a hospital immediately. I could stay with my brother Lane. He lives in New York with his—" she paused, "his lover."

"Be realistic, Laura. What couple wants a third party moving in on them? Do you really think your brother's live-in would welcome another woman?" He finished the last of the pie and pushed the tray off to the side.

Laura stood up. "There wouldn't be another woman in my brother's apartment. I'd be the only one. Lane's *live-in* is a man." Having delivered that pertinent piece of information, she walked away.

Jason was on his feet and at her side a split second later. "Your brother is gay?" An image of future Fletcher family gatherings, kiddie birthday parties, Thanksgiving, Christmas, and the like flashed to mind. His gay brother-in-law, hooker sister-in-law, and his parents at one end of the table, he and Laura and the baby at the other. An ironic smile twisted the corners of his mouth. They certainly would be an updated Norman Rockwell portrait of the ever-changing American family.

"Don't sneer at my brother!" Because so many had, Laura was hypersensitive to anyone's reaction to her brother's homosexuality. She turned on Jason, her eyes a startling, brilliant blue. The subtler shades of green and gray seemed to have been eclipsed. "An arrogant, opinionated, self-centered rake like you has no cause to sneer at anybody."

"I wasn't sneering! And I'm not arrogant, I'm not self-centered, I'm not opinionated, and I'm not a rake." He'd been called all of the above at one time or another, he silently conceded, but never all at once, by the same person. And never by the woman he—

"Oh, ha! You think you're God's gift to women and the world!" Laura snapped. *He'd never intended to see her again.* The pain kept slicing through her. He wouldn't be talking to her now if he wasn't terrified that he'd accidentally impregnated her. If she didn't get away from him, she was going to burst into tears and completely disgrace herself.

Laura fled from the cafeteria, uncaring that her hasty flight had been duly noted and observed by those within.

Jason watched her go, her words ringing in his ears. They stung. Was that really what she thought of him? He tried to work up a self-righteous anger, but a wave of gloom wiped away his efforts.

He passed the director of nursing's office as he

headed toward the elevator. On impulse he went inside, nodding to the secretary before proceeding unannounced into the inner office. Clare Maridian, seated at her desk, looked up from her writing in surprise.

"You've known me for a number of years, Clare," he said brusquely. "One question. Do you think I'm an arrogant, opinionated, self-centered rake who thinks he's God's gift to women and the world?"

"Oh, no!" Clare moaned, clutching her head in her hands. "You made a pass at Laura Novak, she took offense, you had a fight, and now the negotiations with the nursing schools are off."

"Forget about the freakin' nursing schools, Clare. Answer my question."

Clare sighed. "Are you an arrogant, opinionated, self-centered rake who thinks he's God's gift to women and the world? Well, sometimes, I suppose. But you do have a good sense of humor and a sense of fair play that redeems you. And you're a superb doctor. There, does that help?"

Jason abruptly left the office, without saying another word.

As the shifts prepared to change a few minutes before seven the next morning, the night charge nurse told Laura about the pain-racked night that Mrs. Kessler in 601 had spent. The potent narcotic still didn't relieve the pain, and the resident on call who'd been summoned during the night to examine her could find no reason for it.

Laura relayed her concern to Zane Montrose who shrugged impatiently. "Laura, I checked the woman yesterday when you mentioned this and Ken Gruber checked her at three A.M. No one is denying that there is pain after back surgery. There is. But Mrs. Kessler is obviously a hysteric. She's fighting the pain medication and exaggerating the severity of the pain. I can't increase the dosage, Laura, it's already maximum strength. What do you nurses want me to do? Hit the woman over the head and render her unconscious? She wouldn't feel anything then, would she?"

He thrust the chart into Laura's hand and strode away. Seething, Laura waited for Stan Gloz to arrive for rounds. She had no qualms about going over Zane Montrose's head to the next in command.

But when the group assembled for rounds, she was told that Stan was at a conference at Johns Hopkins all day. Laura glanced down at the chart in her hands. Mrs. Kessler's attending physician was Jason Fletcher.

Why did it have to be Jason? Laura railed inwardly. He hadn't spoken to her when he arrived on the floor this morning and she'd been careful to avoid him. She dreaded asking him for anything, even professionally. But she owed it to Mrs. Kessler to do everything in her power to alleviate her patient's discomfort, she reminded herself. Even if it meant considerable discomfort for herself.

She didn't have a chance to speak privately to Jason before they went on rounds with the staff. Mrs. Kessler was weeping and raging when the group entered her room. Laura saw the I-told-you-so looks Zane gave the others.

"The woman is menopausal," Zane said scornfully as the group filed back out into the hall after a few cursory words with Mrs. Kessler. "Wants her husband at her bedside day and night and is throwing a tantrum because he isn't."

"I think the woman is delirious with pain," Laura cut in sharply. "And she isn't being taken seriously."

"We've taken her seriously, Laura," snapped Zane. "We can't spend every minute of the day and night pandering to her."

Jason looked from Zane to Laura. "What's this all about?" he demanded.

"Oh, Mrs. Kessler is running the nurses ragged

with all her complaints and so the nurses are running *us* ragged about her." Zane heaved an exasperated sigh. "She's been thoroughly checked out by Ken Gruber and by me, Dr. Fletcher."

"We think there's something seriously wrong that they've overlooked," Laura retorted. "The Dilaudid isn't alleviating Mrs. Kessler's pain at all—and she's not running us ragged and she's not menopausal or hysterical, either," she finished with a glare at Zane.

"Children, children. No squabbles, please," Jason admonished caustically.

"Jason, will you please check Mrs. Kessler?" Laura implored, ignoring Zane Montrose's gasp of outrage. She suspected she was out of line and decided she didn't care. She was acting in her patient's best interest in her role as Miss Novak, Head Nurse.

Wasn't she? Her eyes met Jason's and a wave of confusion rolled over her. Or was she Laura asking her lover for a favor? For better or worse, their personal and professional relationships seemed inextricably woven together.

Jason cleared his throat. "Has either of you talked this over with Stan Gloz?" he asked diplomatically.

Zane shook his head. "I'm in charge of this patient. There's no need to drag anyone else into the case."

"I planned to talk to Stan, but he's at Johns Hopkins all day today," said Laura. "We can't let Mrs. Kessler suffer for another twenty-four hours, till Stan comes back. She's really in pain, Jason."

Her request called for Jason to take either Zane's side or Laura's and they all knew it. Jason paused, considering. And then said, "I'll see the patient immediately after rounds." So much for diplomacy. As far as he was concerned, Laura had said all the right things and Zane all the wrong ones. He led the group into the next room.

Zane Montrose glowered at Laura until rounds were over and everyone dispersed. Laura ignored him. She accompanied Jason into Mrs. Kessler's room while he examined the patient. She admired his bedside manner; he was kind and reassuring, without a trace of the condescending impatience Zane Montrose had exhibited toward the woman.

"Well, what do you think?" she asked, half running to keep up with his long-legged strides as they left the room and headed toward the nurses' station.

"I don't think the medication has touched her pain," Jason replied briskly. "As far as I can tell there is no physical reason why she should be in pain with regular injections of such a potent analgesic. So we have to look elsewhere for an answer. Open the narcotics cabinet, Laura. I want to have a look at the stock."

They went into the medicine room and Jason closed the door behind them. Laura reached into a drawer and removed the small key to the locked cabinet which held the controlled-substance drugs. After she'd unlocked it, Jason reached inside and removed a box filled with individual vials of Dilaudid, each secured with a small metal seal.

"Do you think something is wrong with the medicine?" Laura asked, astonished. "I hadn't thought of that. It's kept locked up. Everything is signed for and counted at the end of every shift."

"But the key is accessible to anyone who knows where it's kept. And that's common knowledge on the floor." Jason picked up each vial and studied it.

"Look at these." He handed her four of the vials. "Do you see a very slight gap between the center of the seal and the edges in these vials that the others don't have? At first glance nothing looks amiss, but is it possible that someone could have lifted the center of the seal just enough to slip a needle into the rubber stopper and siphon out the drug, replace it with a clear solution—saline, perhaps—and then pressed the seal back in place?"

"But when? How?" Laura paused. "Oh, Jason, I hate to believe someone would deliberately deprive a patient of pain medication for their own—their own fix."

"Or to sell on the streets. It's an ugly prospect." Jason grimaced. "And we don't know if it was tampered with in the pharmacy or here on Six-West. In fact, we don't know for sure if it's been tampered with at all. We'll have to send this lot to a testing lab to be analyzed. I have a friend who works for the DEA. I'll call him right away."

Laura nodded. "And I'll post a new rule concerning the key to the narcotics cabinet. From now on, one person per shift will carry it. I'll keep it on the day shift during the week and the charge nurses on evenings, nights, and all weekend shifts will be responsible for it."

Jason leaned back against the stainless steel counter and folded his arms in front of his chest. "I'll write an order for another narcotic for Mrs. Kessler." He named the drug and dosage. "If it relieves her pain, then this batch is certainly suspect. If not, then I'll order some X rays for her this afternoon."

Laura gazed at him, her eyes sliding over his crisp blue shirt and silk tie, his starched white coat, then lifting to his cleanly shaven jaw, the fine line of his mouth, his gray eyes alert with intelligence and concern under his level black brows.

He was watching her, and her breath caught in her throat. "Thank you, Jason," she said quietly. "For trying to find another reason for Mrs. Kessler's pain. For not dismissing the nursing staff as a bunch of nagging shrews."

Jason smiled slightly. "Yeah, well, even we arrogant, opinionated, self-centered rakes who think we're God's gift to women and the world sometimes have our good moments."

Laura blushed. "I . . . I didn't really mean that," she murmured, looking at the ground. "Sometimes I tend to overreact when it comes to my brother."

"I admit I was—surprised—to hear that your brother was gay but I wasn't sneering about it, Laura."

She gnawed on her lower lip and studied the geometric floor pattern of the tiles. "Growing up gay in a small town like Farview wasn't easy for Lane. Our aunt and uncle were always understanding, but in school the other kids made fun of Lane and the jocks beat him up regularly. He was terribly unhappy. I'm five years younger than he is, but I've always felt—well, protective of him."

"I admire your loyalty to your brother," Jason said softly.

Laura raised her head and their eyes held for a long moment. And then Jason's hands snaked out to catch her wrists and slowly draw her forward until she stood between his legs. She made no move to stop him.

"Have dinner with me tonight, Laura." His hands slid to her hips to anchor her securely against him. "Spend the night with me."

Automatically, her hands went to his chest. To gain leverage to push herself away from him, she assured herself. "No." It didn't come out quite as succinct as she had intended.

He leaned down to nuzzle her neck, his big hands pressing her more tightly into the hard planes of his body. "Yes, baby."

Laura's senses were exploding with pleasure at the feel of his hard body crushed against hers, of his mouth, hot and hard against the sensitive curve of her neck. But even as she responded helplessly to him, she berated herself for it. He didn't care for her; he'd even admitted it! Fighting for control, she wriggled in his grasp. "Let me go, Jason. You said you had no intention of seeing me again and as far as I'm concerned—"

"Forget what I said," Jason said raspily. He'd never felt like this before, confused and frustrated, primitive and possessive. He'd never spent so many hours thinking about one woman, replaying in his mind everything they'd said, everything they'd done. . . .

"Forget about everything but this." He brushed his mouth over hers in a brief, tantalizing caress. "Kiss me, Laura," he breathed. "Open your mouth and kiss me the way you know I want to kiss you. It's what we both want. Give me your tongue. . . ." Fiercely, he covered her mouth with his, his tongue going deep, evoking a hot swell of pleasure within her.

Laura quivered in his arms, moaning into his mouth as she arched against him and gave herself up to his enticing, erotic demands. Her body knew and remembered the delicious pleasure she had found in his arms and submerged every protest her mind presented.

She clung to his broad shoulders, giving his mouth everything it sought, laying claim to him with her own lips and tongue, kissing him as if she had every right to demand everything from him. He'd made her want him in a way she'd never wanted a man before; he took her out of herself, shredding the cloak of deep reserve she used to control herself.

Her effect on him was equally powerful. He'd never wanted these emotional entanglements until he had met Laura. He thought he was immune to that crazy emotional high which caused perfectly sane men to turn their lives upside down.

When he lifted his mouth from hers, she was so weak and trembling she had to cling to him for support. His breathing was ragged and his gray eyes burned with need.

"This is crazy," he murmured huskily. "Necking in the medicine room!" He shook his head slowly. "I didn't even lock the door." He reached over to lock it, but Laura slipped from his arms and reached the door first.

She opened it wide. "I'll draw up the pain medication for Mrs. Kessler while you write the order," she said in a poor imitation of her crisp, brisk nurse-to-doctor tone.

Jason heaved a sigh. They seemed to be locked into a maddening advance-and-retreat strategy. She'd just retreated; now it was time for him to advance. "I'll pick you up at six-thirty tonight," he said resolutely.

Laura prepared the injection for Mrs. Kessler. "I'm not going out with you." She wanted to be with him so much she ached, but not when his motivation was guilt because he thought he'd made her pregnant. She didn't dare delude herself into believing he was beginning to care for her. No, she thought, the moment the possibility of pregnancy was gone, Jason would revert to his original plan, the one he'd decided upon after he'd spent the weekend in bed with her—not to see her again. Laura's face burned. She walked past him, carrying the medication and a packaged alcohol wipe on a small stainless steel tray.

"Six-thirty tonight, Laura," Jason called after her.

She didn't turn around or acknowledge in any way what he'd said.

Eight

Three o'clock in the afternoon was one of the most hectic times on the floor, with the evening staff arriving to join forces with the day staff who didn't leave until three-thirty. Patients were still being transported to and from such places as physical therapy, X ray, and various labs, medical students still abounded, doctors were still writing orders, and visiting hours were in full swing with family members and friends of the patients crowding into the rooms.

"And beginning next week we add the nursing students to all of this," Laura said, marveling as she surveyed the crowded nurses' station. The five weekdays were divided among the three nursing schools with only the weekends being student-free.

"Working nights, I didn't have to deal with visitors or students of any kind," she remarked to the evening charge nurse after finishing the change-of-shift nursing report. "We saw doctors only during emergencies. The floor was so quiet."

"Quiet is something you'll never have when you work daylight," replied the other nurse. "That's why I prefer evenings. The doctors and students are usually gone by five and the visitors leave at eight. Then it's not such a zoo around here. Speaking of zoo—what on earth is that noise? It sounds like . . . like a cheerleading squad?"

They exchanged puzzled glances. "I'll go check," said Laura and headed swiftly down the hall. She bumped into Dana Shakarian, who was on Six-West to work with orthopedic patients unable to be taken down to the physical therapy department. One of those patients was the high school football player, Terry Trice.

"Isn't it terrific?" Dana asked enthusiastically. "Jason Fletcher just got back from his talk at Terry's school and he brought the football coach and the first string varsity and the cheerleading squad with him. You should've seen the look on Terry's face when they came into his room."

Laura felt a quick rush of emotional tears fill her eyes. She swallowed hard and tried to blink them away, but Dana noticed and patted her arm. "I know," she said softly. "Terry gets to me too. It's such a tragedy. I'm just so glad that Jason took the trouble to go over to that school and talk to the students about him. Having kids his own age around means the world to Terry."

Laura nodded, still not trusting herself to speak. She and Dana stood silently for a few moments, listening to the exuberant young voices singing a high school fight song. It was certainly an unusual occurrence on a hospital floor, but Laura knew when to turn a blind eye to the rules.

"We haven't had a chance to talk about the hospital picnic, Laura," Dana said suddenly, casting her a sly smile. "Things worked out for both of us, hmm? You with Jason, me with Zane."

Laura managed to prevent her jaw from dropping. "Jason and me?" she repeated carefully.

"Oh, it's all over the hospital that you two are the latest hot romance," Dana bubbled brightly.

"You've been seen holding hands in the cafeteria, you've been seen arguing, you've been seen disappearing into the medicine room." She laughed. "Everybody is wondering if you're going to be the one to bring the indomitable Jason Fletcher to his knees. Ever since my cousin Sharla married Casey Flynn, that other great Hospital Center heartthrob, the entire staff has been waiting for Jason to fall madly in love too."

Laura was aware that her cheeks were scarlet and she tried in vain to will the color away. "Sorry to disappoint everyone, but Jason Fletcher definitely isn't madly in love with me. The gossip will soon die a natural death."

She was sure of it, especially now. He hadn't yet responded to her page so she'd been unable to convey the news to him that he would never have to bother with her again. She knew how relieved he would be to hear it.

"Don't be so sure of that," Dana said with a grin. "Oh, look, here come Zane and Jason now."

Laura watched Zane Montrose and Jason Fletcher emerge from young Terry Trice's room. Both doctors were smiling. Laura turned to escape to the sanctuary of the nurses' station, but Dana caught her arm. "Wait a sec," she whispered.

Laura did not want to wait. But Dana had delayed her just long enough to make flight on her part look juvenile. Determinedly, she fixed her face into a bland, detached smile as Jason and Zane joined them.

Dana tilted her head, her dark eyes flirtatious. "Hello, Zane."

Zane grinned at her. "I've been looking for you," he said, catching her hand in his. The two of them walked off, leaving Laura and Jason facing each other.

"Looks like you lost your admirer," Jason said, watching the couple's departure. He was inordinately pleased at the thought. "Questioning young Zane's judgment in front of the group this morning and asking me to intervene with Mrs. Kessler put a dent in his pride. If he had any doubts before, that little incident put him firmly in Dana's camp."

"My job here is to see that my patients receive the best care, not to build up any doctor's ego," Laura replied coolly.

Jason arched his brows, his gray eyes gleaming. "A commendable attitude indeed." He moved closer to her. "Now will you please drop the Miss Novak RN smile and smile like Laura for me." His voice was husky, his smile intimate and sexy.

Laura fought the urge to smile back invitingly at him with flirtatious eyes, the way Dana had smiled at Zane. But she didn't. She couldn't. The two relationships were not even remotely similar, she lectured herself sternly. Dana and Zane's romance was just beginning, and flirting and warm smiles were all part of it. As for her and Jason . . . Laura's heart chilled. They'd shared a weekend of what he termed great sex, after which he'd decided never to see her again unless he was forced into it by accidental pregnancy. No, romance, flirtation, and smiles were not for Laura Novak and Jason Fletcher.

Mindful of the hospital gossip and the number of staff milling around, she took a few steps away from him, striving to appear totally and completely professional. "I paged you a little earlier, Dr. Fletcher," she said briskly, treating his request to smile as the piece of acting she considered it to be. "I wanted to tell you two things. One, the medication you ordered for Mrs. Kessler worked like a charm. She's spent a restful day. Would you leave a standing order for her to have it? And—"

"Certainly, Miss Novak." He was still smiling

that heart-stopping smile. "And I believe we can expect the lab analysis of the Dilaudid back in a week or so." He moved closer, eliminating the distance she had created, not taking his eyes from her. "We'll have dinner at my place tonight, Laura. I'll pick up a barbecued chicken and some salads from the deli and— "

"The second thing I wanted to tell you is that there is no reason for any dating charade," Laura interrupted. "You don't have to see me except here at work in the hospital. There aren't going to be any little consequences of this past weekend. I know that for sure now." She blushed and averted her eyes. "I told you I'd let you know as soon as you were safe. Well, you are."

With that, she turned and walked swiftly to the nurses' station. Jason stared after her, absorbing the meaning of her words. There wasn't going to be a little Fletcher. Laura had been right all along—it was the wrong time of the month for her to conceive. They'd taken a risk, but escaped unscathed. There was no need to assuage his conscience, to make any atonement. He was free of her. The Fletcher luck had held and he should be feeling giddy with relief.

But he wasn't. Jason frowned, trying to identify the feeling coursing through him. It was an unfamiliar one, but he was able to recognize it as . . . loss?

Instead of celebrating the continuation of his much-heralded freedom, he felt a strange sense of loss. He stared into space, his mind whirling in confusion. Did that mean he'd wanted a child? True, he had begun to come to terms with the possibility of one, but—

The truth dawned like the proverbial light bulb shining. He wanted the link to Laura that the possibility of pregnancy had provided and now it was broken. The one connection to Laura that he had allowed himself was gone. And he was depressed by the loss.

Cognitive dissonance. He knew the term, he'd even used it today when he'd talked with the high school students. Cognitive dissonance described a state of mind in which conflicting attitudes are held in tension by a person. The students didn't want to believe that someone their age could be lying permanently paralyzed in a hospital bed. At the same time, they wanted to behave compassionately toward their classmate Terry Trice. Jason and the coach had solved their dilemma by not making them choose; they'd *ordered* the students to visit and the kids had been relieved to comply.

Cognitive dissonance, Jason Fletcher style. He wanted the no-ties freedom of his bachelor lifestyle and instinctively knew that it would end if he became involved with Laura Novak. When he'd taken her into his arms for the first time, he realized that she was the one woman who could extract a full commitment from him. And that meant the end of his carefree single life. A threat of pregnancy solved the dilemma by giving him no choice; if Laura were pregnant he *had* to marry her.

But she wasn't, and he didn't have to. He could choose freely. Between Laura and his freedom. Between being a bachelor and a husband. And instead of hauling out his legendary little black book and making a celebratory date tonight with—oh, Heather or perhaps Stefani—he was fighting a disturbing sense of loss because Laura wasn't going to have his baby.

It unsettled him. It worried him. What was he going to do about her?

He was relieved when one of the interns approached him to ask about a possible consultation for one of the patients. Afterward, he went back into Terry Trice's room and joked with Terry and the high school kids there. As long as he kept busy, he didn't have to think about Laura Novak at all.

"Laura, there's someone here to see you, dear!" Aunt Sally's eager voice brought a halt to the rip-roaring volleyball game going on in the backyard.

"Yikes! It's Jason Fletcher!" Lianna exclaimed. "Laura's new flame."

Every eye turned to stare at the tall man in jeans and charcoal gray cotton knit polo shirt who was following Aunt Sally from the back porch.

"He's not my new flame," Laura protested, but she knew that no one was paying any attention to her. They were all too interested in watching Jason walk toward her while Aunt Sally, chatting animatedly, trotted alongside him.

Laura didn't move. It was her turn to serve the ball but she stood right where she was, tense and unsmiling. Jason here? She could hardly believe it. She didn't know what to do or what to say. Having a yardful of relatives witness his arrival made it even more unsettling.

"These are my grandchildren," Aunt Sally told Jason proudly, indicating the seven youngsters, ranging in age from about eight to the midteens, who were lined on either side of the volleyball net. "Laura's cousins," she added. "And my two sons, Jim and Dick and their wives, Margie and Jean, are here, and Lianna, Laura's sister. Come on over and meet Laura's friend Jason Fletcher, everybody," the older woman commanded. They all left their places and crowded around Jason to be introduced.

"You didn't mention that you had a date this evening, Laura." Aunt Sally, small, bright-eyed, and white-haired at sixty-nine, was clearly delighted by Jason's unexpected appearance.

"That's because I didn't have one, Aunt Sal," said Laura. She smiled at her aunt, but carefully avoided glancing at Jason.

"But we did have a date, Laura," Jason inserted smoothly. "I told you I would pick you up at six-thirty, remember? Well, it's a few minutes past six-thirty and here I am."

His eyes flicked over her yellow shorts and matching cotton top. Her hair was pulled high on her head in a ponytail with loose tendrils escaping from the elastic band. Her feet were bare and she wore no makeup. Clearly, she wasn't dressed for a date. His brows narrowed thoughtfully.

"How did you know where I live?" Laura asked, too distracted by the sight of him to play it cool. "Even if you managed to get hold of a Farview phone directory to find their address, you wouldn't know Uncle George and Aunt Sally's last name. It's not Novak."

"It's Bryan," Aunt Sally supplied helpfully. "Laura's mother was my dear little sister Alice."

"As you neglected to give me the necessary information, I asked our mutual friend Dana," said Jason, his voice silky. The way he was looking at her made Laura's skin tingle with excitement. "She picked you up and drove you to the picnic, remember? And she was more than happy to give me directions here."

Laura thought of Dana's gleeful recital of the gossip circulating about her and Jason's "hot new romance." "I wish you hadn't asked Dana," she blurted out. "She'll think—"

"Hey, are we going to play this game or what?" called one of the cousins, a freckle-faced boy about twelve, who was obviously impatient with the interruption.

"Laura, you're not going to leave, are you?" wailed one of the younger children. "You're the best player on our team. We'll lose without you."

"I think she should go right now," Cousin Jim countered jovially. "Then my side will win for sure."

"I'm not going anywhere," Laura assured them all. She cast Jason a sidelong glance. "We're in the midst of the third game of our volleyball tournament and each side has won one game." She reluctantly imparted the information.,

Jason summoned a smile. Though Laura's welcome was as warm as a glacier, her family seemed friendly enough. And he never turned down the chance to participate in any sport, even a backyard family volleyball game. "I'll play," he volunteered heartily.

"Take my place, Jason," said Lianna. "I have to get ready to go to work anyway."

Is that what she called it? Going to work? Jason frowned thoughtfully as he took Lianna's position on the team opposing Laura's. Today Lianna looked young and wholesome, not at all like the hooker he'd believed her to be. She was wearing a shirt and shorts similar to Laura's and her hair was an ash-blond shade which hung long and straight, halfway down her back. It dawned on him that the platinum-and-pink hairstyle horror had been a wig.

"Lianna's a cop with the DC vice squad," Cousin Dick explained. "You should see some of her decoy getups. Why, you'd swear she was a genuine— how shall I say it?—'lady of the streets.'"

"That's exactly what Jason thought Lianna was until this moment," Laura inserted snidely. "He met her dressed for the streets and was aghast."

"Oh, my!" Aunt Sally looked dismayed. As well she might be, Jason thought, an embarrassed flush heating his neck and spreading upward. What sweet little old lady wanted anyone to believe her niece was a hooker? He shot Laura a disapproving glance. She could have at least set him straight about her sister!

"Let's play," begged one of the younger boys and the topic of Lianna was dropped as everybody got into position on either side of the net.

Jason's size, strength, and athletic skills were a boon for his team. Despite Laura's best attempts, he and his team effortlessly defeated her team in the third game of the tournament. And in the fourth and the fifth. His team was officially declared the winners.

"Jason, next time will you be on our team?" asked one of the little girls who'd been on Laura's.

Jason tweaked her long, brown braid. "Sure will, princess."

Laura declined to mention that there would be no next time. She still didn't know what he was doing here. He had fit in well with her family, but that was probably because they were as serious about playing and winning as he was. And, except for those first initial moments, he'd paid no attention to her, concentrating instead on the volleyball game. It was sort of a replay of the day they'd met, except the hospital softball game had been the focus of his attention then.

"Grandpa is back with the ice cream," Aunt Sally said to her grandchildren. "Why don't you kids go into the kitchen and scoop out the flavors you want." She grinned at the adults. "He bought six different kinds. And Jason, you haven't met Laura's uncle George yet." Aunt Sally took Jason's arm to lead him into the kitchen where the kids were already attacking the ice cream with colored plastic scoops.

Laura felt obliged to follow them.

Uncle George seemed thrilled to meet "Laura's friend, Jason" and if he recalled that he'd originally believed Dr. Jason Fletcher to be a "nice old doc," he made no mention of it.

"Have you worked up an appetite for dinner, Laura?" Jason turned to Laura with one of his most engaging smiles. Warm, intimate, sexy. He'd smiled that smile when she'd been in his bedroom. A bittersweet rush of pain mingled with desire attacked her.

"I already ate dinner," she said flatly, steeling herself against the magic he so easily wove around her.

"This was a *dinner* date you didn't know you had, Laura? Does that mean you haven't eaten yet, Jason?" Aunt Sally was concerned; she hated to see anyone miss a meal. "Here, let me fix you something. We had roast beef tonight. I'll warm some up for you—and some gravy and potatoes and carrots and biscuits too. It'll just take a few minutes. Please, go sit down in the dining room, both of you." Placing one hand on Laura's back and the other on Jason's, she gave each a gentle shove in the direction of the dining room.

Since everyone else was crowded into the kitchen, it was quiet in the dining room. And very private. Laura glanced nervously around, silently willing some of her younger cousins to come charging in. They didn't.

"I like your family," Jason said at last. Laura wouldn't look at him. Her big eyes were darting everywhere but in his direction. "Your aunt and uncle are great. Your cousins, too. All the kids . . ." His voice trailed off and he started walking toward her.

"I have a wonderful family," Laura agreed, watching him with round, wary eyes. Reflexively, she took a few steps backward.

Jason arched his brows, his smile lightly mocking, as he continued his advance. "I'll admit it came as something of a relief to learn that your sister is an upstanding citizen—on the police force, no less."

Too late, Laura became aware of his strategy. He had backed her against the wall and stood directly in front of her, his hands in the pockets of his jeans. He towered over her, close, but not quite touching her body with his. The masculine size and strength of him, the warmth of his body heat, and the scent of his after-shave filled her senses. Her head began to spin.

"Jason, why did you come here tonight?" she whispered tremulously.

"Don't you know, Laura?" Slowly, carefully, he rested his lower body against hers, his hands still in his jeans pockets.

Laura felt the hard power of his erection against her and drew in a sharp breath. "No, I don't know." She pressed her head back against the wall and tried to slow the fierce thudding of her heart. "Now that there isn't any reason for you to—oh!" She broke off in a gasp when his mouth brushed hers.

"No reason?" Jason nibbled on her lips as he talked to her. "Doesn't the fact that I'm crazy about you qualify?" He didn't lift his mouth, but kept his lips against hers while he spoke in a husky whisper. "I want you, Laura. More than I've ever wanted any woman."

"But—But you said—" she tried to turn her head from side to side, but he kept his mouth lightly on hers, teasing her with tiny, biting little kisses. His thigh slipped between hers, but still he kept his hands in his pockets, making no attempt to hold her.

"What did I say, sweetheart?"

Laura felt him smile against her lips. Her eyelids closed heavily and the tip of her tongue slipped into his mouth before she was fully aware of what she was doing. She closed her fingers around his wrists, wanting to pull his hands from his pockets. She wanted to feel them on her, she wanted him to hold her, to caress her.

"Tell me everything you think I said," he coaxed sexily.

He continued to tease her with the maddening, staccato touch of his lips against hers, not lifting his mouth from her mouth but not kissing her deeply. Or allowing her to deepen their kisses either. When he didn't remove his hands from his pockets she gave up the effort, sliding her hands along his arms to his shoulders instead. Clutching him, she brought herself fully against him, and a soft moan escaped her throat when her breasts impacted against the solid muscular strength of his chest.

"You said you didn't want to see me again," she said breathlessly. It was hard enough to think coherently, let alone to speak. He wouldn't let her mouth leave his; it was dizzying to talk while their mouths were touching, her lips moving against his.

"And you believed me?" He laughed softly, and the sound of it and the feel of it sent sensual darts shooting along her spine.

"You said one weekend with me was enough for you." Her voice caught. "You wouldn't have seen me or even talked to me again if we both weren't working on Six-West."

His tongue traced the outline of her lips. "But since we are, the point is moot, isn't it, Laura?" He moved his hips, slightly, subtly, and Laura whimpered at the force of desire that rippled through her.

Her fingers gripped his shoulders convulsively. "Don't tease me, Jason," she pleaded. She felt exposed and vulnerable. She had no defenses against him; he'd successfully obliterated the last vestiges of her self-control. "You were afraid I was pregnant, but I'm not and—"

"And you need to have it spelled out for you, don't you, honey?" He moved his mouth to her neck and began to kiss her there.

The touch of his lips on the sensitive curve of

her neck electrified her. She was aroused and aching. His sensual teasing had set every nerve ending aflame.

"I woke up on Monday morning and realized that I'd fallen hard for you," Jason continued, nuzzling her.

His words sent a thrill of joy quivering through Laura. The way he was looking at her, the way he couldn't bear to let her mouth leave his, not even while they spoke, made her confidence soar. She drew back a fraction and gazed up at him through her lashes. "How hard?" she murmured throatily and moved provocatively against the rock-hard evidence of his desire.

His eyes glinted in response to her sexual teasing. "Real hard, baby." He took his hands from his pockets at last and wrapped her in his arms. "Every time I'm near you, every time I think of you . . ." His voice was soft in her ear, his teeth gently biting her soft lobe.

Laura sighed and lay against him, luxuriating in his warm strength. She was overwhelmed by the depth of her feelings for him and by the force of the feminine hunger he'd awakened in her. And then there was the giddy relief at being back in his arms that made her want to laugh with elation and cry with emotional tears, all at the same time.

"Oh, Jason, I wish you would've told me all this on Monday," she whispered. She remembered how much she'd wanted to go to him that morning, how much she'd needed to be cuddled and reassured. But he had looked so forbidding and her own feelings of shame and consternation had overpowered her from seeking what she needed from him.

"I couldn't have told you, honey. Not then. I felt trapped, Laura. I was running scared."

"And—And now you're not?"

His big hands moved over her, caressing her, pressing her closer, molding her curvy softness to the hard planes of his body. "It finally occurred to me that if I was caught in a trap, you weren't bent on keeping me there. In fact you were determined to set me free." He kissed the top of her head and she tilted her head back and gazed up at him. "You could have let me go on believing that you were pregnant," he said quietly. "I would've married you, you know."

"Jason, that's not only unconscionable, it's impossible." Her eyes sparked with tiny blue flames. "You certainly would notice when there was no baby nine months from now."

"You're too honest to be devious, aren't you, little one?" Jason regarded her with intense, serious eyes. "There are several things you could've done after I'd married you. Pretended to have a convenient alleged miscarriage. Or actually become pregnant once the ring was safely on your finger. But you didn't choose to go either route, Laura."

Laura shuddered. "I should say not! I don't want to be with anyone who"—she stared up at him with searching eyes—"who doesn't want to be with me." She stood on tiptoe to press her mouth to his at the same moment that Aunt Sally bustled into the room.

"Here's your dinner, Jason, dear. Oops, excuse me, I'll just— "

Jason turned his head but kept Laura anchored firmly against him. "Thanks, Aunt Sal. I'm starved."

Aunt Sally was positively beaming with delight at the sight of her niece in Jason Fletcher's arms. Laura blushed and concentrated on watching her aunt place the food and some silverware on a cloth mat on the table.

"That looks delicious," Jason said enthusiastically. He eased into a chair, successfully concealing his burgeoning arousal. Laura sat down beside him. She caught his eye and they exchanged sheep-ish grins.

"It is delicious," he proclaimed, after sampling a forkful.

Aunt Sally made her departure, her expression both satisfied and speculative as she cast a final glance at the couple.

"I saw you wolf down that awful meal in the hospital cafeteria with the same gusto," Laura teased. "You obviously have a very healthy appetite."

"Oh, I do." The smile he gave her was outrage-ously suggestive.

Jason reached over to take Laura's hand in his and rub his thumb over her palm. "You're no slouch in the appetite department, either, sweet-heart. I remember how ravenous you were when I was feeding you that ravioli on Sunday." His gray eyes swept over her in a hot, needy glance. "Not to mention later that night when I put something else in—"

"Jason!" Laura flushed scarlet.

He laughed huskily. "Who could guess that starched, proper Miss Novak is fantastic in bed? Passionate, adventurous." His voice lowered and he stared into her eyes. "Honest and sweet. Loving. And I'm the only man who knows that Miss Novak the perfect nurse is also Laura the perfect lover."

His evocative words thrilled the sensuous woman in her, but the element of cautious reserve in her character was too deeply ingrained to forget the hospital gossip already building around the two of them. "Jason, you won't talk about me?" It was both an uncertain question and a heartfelt plea.

"What do you mean, Laura?" The teasing note was gone. His gray eyes were serious, the amused glint vanishing.

"I've always hated being a topic of discussion. Probably because I've been one so often. For years after my parents died, my sister and brother and I were 'the poor little Novaks' to everyone in Farview. Then everyone began whispering about Lane and speculating how difficult it must be for Lianna and me to have 'such a brother.' Then Danny was killed and I was the 'tragic bride.' "

She gnawed anxiously on her lower lip. "I don't want to be known throughout the Hospital Center as 'Jason Fletcher's current flame.' " Or worse, one of Jason Fletcher's rejects, she thought but didn't say.

"Laura, I've provided the hospital with a lot of hot gossip, so a relationship with me guarantees that you'll get yourself talked about." He lifted her hand to his mouth and pressed his lips to her palm. "But I won't be supplying information to anyone, honey. You can trust me on that. I want what's between us to remain private."

His feelings for her were much too strong and too personal to divulge to others. And there was something else. Somehow the belief that Laura belonged to him had taken root; he felt protective and possessive of her and everything they shared. The doctrine of sexual exclusivity, previously inconceivable to him, now seemed entirely correct.

He kept her hand in his while he finished eating. Conversation was light and desultory, but a taut sexual tension stretched between them.

"Am I right in assuming that you aren't coming home with me tonight?" Jason asked, pushing the empty plate aside and rising to his feet. Since he was still holding her hand, she rose with him.

"Tonight?" Laura felt a flood of hot color heat her cheeks. "But I told you that I—"

"I understand that you have a few inhibitions to overcome," Jason interrupted with a wicked smile. "And you will, in time. But this evening we'll find something to do in Farview. *Is* there anything to do in Farview?"

"We have a movie theater that plays second-run movies."

"What's playing tonight?"

When she named a well-known Disney cartoon classic, Jason chuckled and shook his head. "Let's pass on that. Anywhere else to go in this town?"

"We have an ice cream place that doubles as a teenage hangout."

"Forget it. After spending hours with Terry Trice's classmates today, I'm ready for a break from the teen set. And if you want ice cream, your uncle George has six different flavors in the kitchen." His eyes gleamed. "Does Farview have a notorious lovers' lane where everybody goes to park and make out?"

"Jason Fletcher! What a question!"

"Well, is there such a place?"

She put her arms around his waist and pressed her forehead against the soft cotton of his shirt. Her face was hot. "Yes," she replied in a muffled voice.

"And will you show me where it is?"

His chest rumbled with soft laughter that reverberated against her cheek. "Yes," she whispered.

"Let's go." He took her hand and led her out to the kitchen where he informed her family that they were "going for a drive." An exultant chorus of "Have a good time!" followed them out the door.

"This is slightly embarrassing," Laura said with a rueful smile. "You're the first man who's come to the house to see me since Danny's death and my family is making it incredibly obvious that they're thrilled."

"Don't worry about it. I'm used to being worshipped," Jason kidded. "My parents keep my boyhood room as a shrine."

"Your very spoiled. And very experienced," Laura said thoughtfully.

"And you're neither." His gray eyes challenged her. "Think you can handle me?"

"I don't know," she said frankly. "I'm a rather

unsophisticated small-town girl who's directed most of my energy into performance, first in school, then at the hospital."

Jason smiled. "Let me assure you that the energy you directed toward your performance in bed is worthy of a five-star rating if there were a sexual Michelin guide."

"Then I'll have to answer *maybe* I can handle you," Laura said, getting into the spirit of it all. "I'm good in bed and you want me sexually."

"Oh, yes, Laura," Jason agreed, his voice deep and low. "I most certainly want you. But not only sexually," he added with a thoughtful frown. "That's why I'm here."

"Because you want more from me than great sex?"

It was true, but he wasn't ready to admit it yet. Not to her or to himself. Jason quickly switched the subject. "We'll go in your car. With the bucket seats and gear shift, the Jag is not designed for parking."

He hadn't answered her question, Laura noted. And by not tossing off some flippant line, he'd revealed more than he intended. She was suddenly buoyed by a flash of optimism. *Yes, I can handle you, Jason Fletcher,* she told herself and suddenly, she almost believed it.

She showed him her car, a bright yellow Ford Escort, and he teased her about the color, saying that she would probably be mistaken for a taxicab in the city. He was content to let her drive and she gave him a brief tour of Farview, which didn't take long because the town was so small. Her heart was racing and her pulses jumping when she pulled onto Pritchard Road, the notorious stretch of secluded woods just outside the Farview town limits. She noted with relief that there were no other cars parked there.

Turning off the engine, she stared through the

windshield at the sun setting through the trees. "You probably had a place reserved for you at your old hometown parking spot, but this is the first time I've ever parked on Pritchard Road."

"Somehow that doesn't surprise me." Jason pulled her across the seat into his arms. "I'm glad your first time—all of your first times—are with me." He covered her breast with his big hand as his mouth lowered to hers. "You're mine, Laura."

She thrilled to the possessiveness in his voice and his caressing hands, to the ardent hunger of his mouth. *Yes, I'm yours, Jason,* she silently vowed to him. *I belong to you completely because I'm in love with you.* But she didn't dare tell him. First he'd mentioned feeling dutiful toward her, next he'd talked of his desire for her. But the word love hadn't been mentioned and she was too uncertain of him to bring it up first.

Their kisses grew deeper and more impassioned. The confines of the small car and the barrier of their clothes imposed maddening frustrations. "Jason, Jason, please," Laura cried. The words slipped out reflexively, although she wasn't even sure what she was pleading for. Satisfaction for the passionate hunger coursing through her? Or the words of love she yearned to hear? Both, perhaps.

"I know, honey, I know,"Jason said soothingly, holding her still but tightly against him. "I'd forgotten that parking is hell on the nerves. We need to calm down and cool off." He stroked her hair lightly, dropping an occasional kiss on the top of her head.

"Yes," she said shakily. "Hell on the nerves." A neat turn of phrase that also accurately summed up her relationship to date with Jason. She'd known him less than a week, yet he'd evoked more intense and acute emotional reactions in her than she'd experienced in her entire tranquil and easy relationship with poor Danny.

It was exhilarating, and it was scary. She was

taking a great emotional risk by giving herself so completely to a man with a romantic track record like Jason's and she knew it. Strange, but she'd always been one to avoid such risks. In her experience, life was dangerous enough; veering from the safety of reserved control into the precarious realm of emotional risk and chance was sheer folly. But she was in love with Jason. And that gave her the courage to break out of the restraints of caution and control and plunge into the turbulent seas of love.

Nine

Jason drove to Farview to see Laura and visit with her family every evening for the rest of the week, except Friday when he was called into the Shock/Trauma Unit's operating room to try to surgically repair the shattered pelvis of a twenty-year-old girl who had been thrown from a car when it struck a tree.

"It was hellish in that OR tonight," Jason said wearily when he called Laura late that night from the dark solitude of his bedroom. "While I worked on the girl, we had a neurosurgeon at her head to deal with her skull fracture and Case Flynn trying to repair lacerations of her liver and kidneys and remove her spleen which had ruptured."

Laura shivered. "Do you think she's going to make it?" she asked quietly.

"I don't know." Jason shook his head. "I just don't know. Her condition is critical. The helicopter got her to us within the golden hour, but with the extent of her injuries, it's too early to tell."

Laura knew the "golden hour" he referred to was the crucial time span following critical injury when the effects of shock could still be reversed.

SIMPLY IRRESISTIBLE • 143

"Such a young girl," Laura murmured. "Oh, Jason, it's such a shame."

Jason cleared his throat. "It's a damn shame, Laura. Talking to her family afterward was . . . rough."

It was a pallid word to describe the almost indescribably painful scene. His voice trailed off. There were times when the enormity of the tragedies he encountered was difficult to bear. Previously he'd sought refuge in fast, mind-blotting pleasures. But tonight he'd elected to return to his dark, quiet house and call Laura. He wanted her so badly; he ached for the life-affirming warmth of her body.

"I wish I were there with you, Jason," Laura said softly, echoing his thoughts. "If I leave now, I can be at your place within the hour."

For the first time, his concern for a woman overrode his lust for her. "Sweetheart, as much as I want you here, I'll have to settle for the sound of your voice tonight. I don't want you on the roads at this hour."

"Jason, do you think you could come here?" Laura asked, and the hesitancy in her voice made him smile.

"I want to make love to you, Laura," he said huskily. "And I know you well enough to know that you couldn't make love with your aunt and uncle sleeping a few doors away." He gave a soft laugh. "I harbor no such inhibitions, but I do respect yours." Another first for him.

"And parking on Pritchard Road is out of the question," he continued. "I can't handle the frustration of another hot, unconsummated necking session. Not tonight."

The mention of those nightly sessions sent a frisson of heat through Laura. "I've decided to look for an apartment tomorrow, Jason," she told him. "I've been thinking about it all week. It's time for me to leave home and find a place of my own."

She was no longer a grieving young girl; she was a woman with a good job and a man she loved. The future no longer loomed fearful and lonely; it was exciting and full of possibilities.

"Dana told me there's a vacancy in the building where one of her cousins lives," she continued. "It's near the Hospital Center and the rent is supposed to be reasonable. She said a lot of hospital people live there. I thought I'd check it out first thing in the morning."

"I'll meet you there." Jason surprised himself by offering. Now why had he done that? he wondered, grimacing. Apartment hunting wasn't his bag; he'd never even looked for his own place, preferring to have someone else—a willing girlfriend, the hospital housing office, a real estate agent, whomever—find a suitable place for him to live. And he'd intended to sleep late tomorrow morning.

"Oh, you don't have to do that, Jason. My appointment with the landlord is early, at eight o'clock, and you'll want to sleep in tomorrow."

"I know I don't *have* to, Laura." But suddenly he wanted to, very much. "Give me the address and I'll be there at eight."

"I hate this place," Jason declared, gazing around the small, two-room apartment. They'd spent the last ten minutes examining the available apartment, then the landlord had retired discreetly to the hall to await their decision.

"I like it!" Laura said enthusiastically, lifting the shade to look out the window. A twenty-four-hour convenience store was on the corner, directly across the street.

"Laura, it's too small, the building is too old, and the neighborhood isn't safe."

"The landlord says that all the apartments on

the block are rented by students or hospital personnel," Laura reminded him. "And the location is perfect. It's close enough to the Hospital Center to walk on nice days."

"The very next block borders an area of decaying rowhouses where every problem known to social services exists, not to mention crime. Laura, I've operated on two gunshot wounds that occurred within three blocks of here."

"It's cozy and cute and I can afford the rent," Laura said with determination. "I already have some ideas on how to fix it up. And Lianna says that there's potential danger in any part of any big city, but if you're alert and aware and careful, your chances of being a victim of crime are lessened."

"Of course she'd say that. She's with the metropolitan police department. They *have* to say things like that. They could hardly come out and admit that it's dangerous to walk down the city streets in broad daylight, even if it's true. It would be a reflection on the police force."

"You're very cynical, Jason," Laura said reprovingly.

"And you're very naive. I can't let you move into this place." He set his jaw determinedly. "I have an idea. You can move in with me, Laura. I have plenty of room, the development provides its own security, and—you won't have to pay any rent. Think of the money you'll be able to save!"

Laura laughed. She couldn't help it. "Oh, Jason, you should hear yourself. You sound like a combination overprotective parent and real estate agent."

"This isn't a joke, Laura," he said stiffly. Missing completely was his usual blasé, laissez-faire attitude. "It's the first time I've ever asked anyone to live with me and I don't find anything funny about it. Nor is there a bit of humor in you contemplating living in this dump."

She crossed the room to wrap her arms around him. "I appreciate your concern for my safety, Jason," she said softly. "And for my bank account too." Her lovely eyes danced. "But I can't move in with you."

She felt soft, warm, and feminine. Jason held her close. It felt so good and so right to have her in his arms. "Why can't you?" he demanded huskily. "Are you afraid your aunt and uncle might not approve?"

"Are you kidding? Aunt Sally and Uncle George like you so much they'd gladly help me move into your place today if I asked. But I'm not the live-in lover type, Jason." Laura gazed up at him earnestly. "And I don't think you are either, although for reasons different from mine. Having someone around your house all the time would get on your nerves. You value your privacy and your freedom too much."

"Dammit, Laura, I'm not proposing that you be my roommate!" His gray eyes hardened. "And I'm not proposing marriage, either. That's the real issue here, isn't it? If I asked you to marry me, you'd be loading up the U-Haul trailer faster than—"

"We haven't known each other long enough to get married," Laura interrupted calmly. "Anyway, I need the experience of having a place of my own. It takes independence and courage and maturity to live alone, and I want to prove—"

"—to yourself that you possess all three," Jason finished with a wry smile. His flash of anger had already faded. Laura was not manipulative, he reminded himself. She'd already proven her honesty to him. "And having made it a test of character, you're determined to succeed . . . not only to succeed but to excel."

She smiled. "Something like that, I suppose. I'm going to tell the landlord that I want to sign the lease, Jason."

Jason was not pleased. It came as something of a shock to realize that he couldn't control Laura, that she was going to do what she wanted rather than what he told her to do. If he gave her an order on Six-West as physician to nurse, she would obey it to the letter. He regretted that he couldn't seem to exert that same power here and now.

His displeasure was heightened when Laura decided to move into her new apartment immediately. He'd planned to spend the day with her in his bed—and he was prepared to insist on it. "I'm not spending my weekend making trips back and forth to Farview and up and down the three flights of stairs in this building," he said testily.

"Oh, I don't expect you to, Jason," Laura exclaimed, her eyes wide with concern. "My sister and my cousins offered to help, and Aunt Sally and Uncle George, too. I wouldn't dream of asking you to give up your free time for something as tedious as moving!"

"You don't expect me to help, but your seventy-year-old uncle will be tramping up and down all those stairs? Your sister has been working the night shift all week and is supposed to sleep during the day, but she's been recruited to help? Why should I be exempt?" For reasons he couldn't begin to fathom, Jason was incensed. And from that moment, he was absolutely adamant about helping Laura move into her new apartment.

Aunt Sally and Uncle George commented on the friendly atmosphere in the building as they helped Laura unpack her dishes, pots, and pans in the miniscule kitchen. All day long, while Jason, Lianna, and various members of the family helped to move Laura in, tenants from the other apartments dropped by. Aunt Sally had coffee, sodas, and plenty of her homemade cookies on hand to welcome the visitors who all stayed to chat awhile.

"You're going to love it here, Laura!" exclaimed dark-haired, sparkling-eyed Beth Shakarian, a nurse in the Hospital Center's labor and delivery suite. She lived on the floor below. "Everybody in the building works at the Hospital Center and we're all single and we have parties all the time. In fact my roommate Sarah, who works in the OR, and I are having a party tonight. Everybody is supposed to bring something, but since you're new, you don't have to. Please come!"

"Laura and I already have plans for tonight," Jason inserted coolly. Though he hadn't discussed it with Laura, he assumed she knew she would be spending the evening with him.

Jason saw Beth stare from him to Laura. It rankled him a little that Beth hadn't noticed him until now. He knew she was the ingenue type who stuck with guys her own age, but did she have to look so incredulous at the notion that Laura would be seeing him tonight? Furthermore, Beth's description of life in this building disturbed him. She made it sound like a coed dorm—or even worse, a lively singles' complex. Such a place was fine for Beth and her roommate and everybody else who lived here, but not for Laura! He didn't want her eternally partying with a bunch of kids in their twenties; the very thought chilled him.

"You can come to the party too, Dr. Fletcher," Beth said politely, addressing him in the same respectful tones she'd used upon meeting Uncle George.

Dana Shakarian chose that moment to make her arrival, peering into the open door from the hall and then rushing in at the sight of Laura. "Laura, you did it! You moved here!" she squealed and threw her arms around Laura. "I'm so excited for you! Oh, I see you already met my cousin Beth. Did she invite you to her party tonight?"

"She can't come," Beth interjected. "She has a date with Dr. Fletcher."

Dana whirled around to face Jason. "Aw, come on, Jason," she said in a teasing, wheedling tone.

"Let Laura come to the party. It'll be a great opportunity for her to meet all her new neighbors. Everybody in the building is coming and bringing friends."

Laura's eyes met Jason's. He looked irked and she wondered why. From what she'd heard, Jason Fletcher was always game for a party.

Jason Fletcher, that fabled party animal, known for his spontaneity—he would change plans, arrangements, and dates at the blink of an eye—shook his head. "Sorry, Dana. We can't make it. As I said, we have other plans," he said in a tone that brooked no more argument.

"Some other time then," Beth inserted diplomatically.

"Zane and I are going grocery shopping at the Giant," said Dana. "Can we pick up anything for you, Laura? What about you, Beth?" Both girls shook their heads.

"Zane Montrose lives next door to me on the second floor," Beth explained to Laura. She smiled at her cousin. "Since Dana started going out with him, she's always around."

"Montrose lives here?" Jason wasn't happy to hear that. Especially since Laura and Zane had patched up their brief feud over Mrs. Kessler. But if Dana shared his qualms about having Laura in the building, she didn't show it. She cheerfully called good-bye and sauntered out the door. Beth left a few minutes later.

"What are your special plans for tonight, Jason?" one of Laura's teenage cousins asked curiously.

Jason felt all eyes on him. "I made dinner reservations at Jean-Louis, in the Watergate," he said smoothly, vowing to slip across the street to the pay phone and make the reservations at once.

"Oh, that's a lovely place," Aunt Sally said gaily. "I hear the food is wonderful. And it's supposed to be very fancy. You'll have to wear something special, Laura."

Jason smiled and nodded. "If you'll excuse me for a few minutes, I need to pick up, uh, a copy of this week's *TV Guide* at the store across the street." He left the apartment so quickly, he didn't notice Laura following him.

The telephone directory had been stolen from its moorings in the phone booth, so he dialed information to get the number of the restaurant. The only table available all evening was at the somewhat unfashionable hour of six forty-five, but Jason took it gratefully. Smiling with satisfaction, he stepped from the phone booth—and saw Laura standing directly in front of him.

"I came to buy a *TV Guide*, too," she said. She looked puzzled. "You just made the reservations at the restaurant?"

It was one of the few times in his life that Jason was thoroughly nonplussed. The other times had been with Laura as well. "Yes," he admitted. Now she knew he'd been lying when he'd told the others she couldn't go to the party. If she ripped into him, it was nothing less than he deserved and he knew it. He braced himself.

A smile played across Laura's face and her eyes lit with humor, heightening the beautiful, unusual shade. "Did you really intend to take me to this restaurant and forgot to make the reservations, or is this an elaborate excuse to avoid attending that party?"

Jason felt relief surge through him. The force of it made him aware of how much he hadn't wanted them to quarrel. He marveled at the power she possessed over his emotions. It was as astonishing as it was daunting to a man who was used to having it all his way. "A little of both, perhaps," he said reluctantly. He took her hand in his and tucked it into his pocket. "After all, I haven't taken you anywhere—not even out for an ice cream cone in Farview. It's about time I took you somewhere ridiculously expensive."

"So you can demand payment at the end of the evening for all the money you've spent?" Laura accused teasingly.

Jason laughed. "You'd better believe it."

They started back to the apartment building, their hands linked in his pocket, their shoulders brushing familiarly.

When they were inside the vestibule, he pulled her into his arms. "You're spending the night with me tonight, Laura. Pack whatever you think you'll need and we'll take it with us when we leave for the restaurant."

Holding hands, they walked up the three flights of stairs, Jason jokingly complaining about the lack of elevators all the way. He stopped her a few feet before they reached her apartment. "Laura, about that party . . . You were right, I didn't want to go. I wanted to be alone with you tonight, not share you with an apartment full of rollicking bozos."

"From what I've heard, you've always been one of the most eager rollicking bozos, ever ready to party."

She was right, of course. "Yeah, well . . ." He shrugged and quickly shepherded her inside her apartment. He felt totally shaken. He had almost uttered the words he never thought he'd have to say about himself; he'd liked himself so much the way he had always been. But the unspoken words *I've changed* bounced around his brain, as revealing and potent as if he'd actually said them aloud.

Another thought, equally disturbing, struck him—suddenly the idea of spending a quiet evening at home didn't seem so bad. Not if Laura were spending it with him. Even if she were wearing a flannel robe and sweat socks!

• • •

"You look beautiful tonight," Jason said to Laura as they held hands across the candlelit table at posh Jean-Louis in the exclusive Watergate complex.

"I borrowed this dress from Lianna," Laura confessed. "When Aunt Sal told her you were taking me here, she insisted on bringing it right over to my apartment."

The dress was white silk with a short, flared skirt, long, tight sleeves, and an off-the-shoulder neckline with a few spangles of white sequins across the bust.

"I'm glad she didn't offer you that getup she was wearing the first time I met her." Jason rolled his eyes heavenward.

Laura grinned. "Poor Jason, you were so shocked." The memory of that encounter now struck her as hilarious. "There you were, terrified that you'd made me pregnant and would have to marry me, and then you're confronted with my sister you mistook for a hooker! Not at all the sort of family you visualized marrying into, I'm sure."

Jason, remembering the sinking panic of that day, gave his head a rueful shake and attempted to divert her attention to the menu.

But Laura, perhaps buoyed by two glasses of expensive French wine, continued to tease him. "I can just imagine your horror. I bet you pictured your future wife to be some cool, stylish debutante with an impeccable family background, old money, and all the right social connections."

Jason said nothing. She'd come uncomfortably close to the truth on that one. An unwelcome combination of guilt and confusion made him scowl. The imaginary aloof deb was a far cry from the warm, passionate, utterly irresistible woman sitting across the table from him. He knew he should tell her so; she was undoubtedly waiting to hear the words.

Feeling perverse and stubbornly fighting for his bachelor life, he remained silent.

Laura gazed at him in the candlelight. She'd never seen him dressed up before and he looked devastatingly attractive in a dark charcoal gray European-cut suit. Sophisticated, sought-after, and rich, and ultimately unavailable to the Laura Novaks of this world. The realization hurt. How had she managed to let herself forget it, even for a moment? Some of the brightness faded from her eyes and she withdrew her hand from his, ostensibly to hold the large menu more easily.

Jason watched her, sensing her reserve and guessing at the cause. He heaved an impatient sigh. "Laura, I've always made it a point to avoid discussing marriage, even hypothetically, because it invariably leads to—er, misunderstandings."

"You've already discussed marriage hypothetically. In the Hospital Center cafeteria over meat loaf and mashed potatoes, remember?" she asked lightly, caustically. "I know I'll never forget it."

His mouth tightened. He didn't care for the sarcastic direction this conversation had taken. "That was due to—er—extenuating circumstances."

"Of course. I understand." She flashed a brilliant smile which he knew was both fixed and false. "What appetizer do you recommend?"

"I recommend that you don't go into a snit because I didn't contradict your debutante theory with a description of you as my idea of the perfect wife."

His perception unnerved her, and embarrassed her too. Laura silently cursed the telltale blush which pinked her cheeks. "I'm not in a snit. I'm hungry." She could be as maddeningly evasive as he if the occasion demanded. "I think I'll try the escargots in puff pastry," she said, striving for a nonchalance she was far from feeling. "That's something I can't make at home."

She was giving him the chance to conduct the evening on a totally superficial level. His favorite kind of evening. All he had to do was to make some innocuous, impersonal remark about the food or the wine or French cooking in general.

Instead, his expression intense, he plucked the menu from her fingers and took both her hands in his. "All right, if you want to discuss my theoretical ideal marriage partner—"

"I'd rather discuss the menu," Laura countered flippantly.

He ignored that and plunged ahead. "Socio-economic background aside, the woman I marry will be someone I choose logically and rationally with no messy emotions cluttering up my mind. She'll be someone who'll be content to go her own way while I go mine, someone who will make no demands on me and who will be satisfied with the part of myself allotted to her." There, he'd said it! Jason sat back in his chair, his gray eyes blazing.

"You should get a cat," retorted Laura. "The relationship you've just described would suit one perfectly. And if you do marry a woman like that, you'll deserve all the unhappiness you're sure to get."

"Aren't you going to share your conception of the ideal marriage partner?" he challenged.

"Well, it's the polar opposite of yours. Unlike your emotions, mine will be completely engaged by the person I marry. We might have different hobbies or interests, but we'll share the same values and we'll enjoy and appreciate our time together. As for making demands on each other, why, that goes with the territory. Marriage allows you to make demands on each other and to have them met. And my husband and I won't parcel ourselves out in stingy little packages. I'll have all of him and he'll get all of me."

Jason listened to her, transfixed. It took a moment for the fact that she'd stopped speaking to register with him. "I see," was all he could manage to say.

Laura felt a surge of hostility sweep through

her. She would never be the icy princess he claimed to want; his expectations of marriage were downright chilling. Falling in love with him was the most stupid thing she'd ever done, she scolded herself. Laura, the perfectionist who'd spent most of her life trying to do everything exactly right, did not like feeling stupid.

Even worse, she found it impossible to slip behind the controlled mask of composure she'd spent years perfecting. Since Jason had come into her life, she was unable to repress the emotions that churned within her. Right now it was anger.

"Since neither of us is what the other wants, it's a good thing that we're simply having an affair," she snapped, snatching her menu from him.

"Are we having an affair? In my experience, having an affair means sleeping together, something we haven't done all week."

"And we're not going to do it tonight, either." She stood up, her blue-green-gray eyes flashing. "I'm calling a taxi and going home."

"If you go running off, I won't come after you, Laura."

"Good!" She stalked from the restaurant, her head held high.

Jason sat at the table alone for a few minutes. It was by no means the first time in his life he'd had a fight with his date that culminated in the woman storming off. But the desolation which swept over him was brand-new. Decisively, he rose from the table and went into the vestibule of the restaurant, where he found Laura standing, staring out the open door.

The skies were gray and rain was beginning to fall. "Laura," he began.

"I'm waiting for my cab. They said it would be here shortly," she said coldly, turning her back to him.

He stared at the smooth bare curve of her shoulders, the vulnerable softness of her nape. He closed his eyes, staggered by the driving desire roaring through him. "You can't go," he said thickly. "Your—Your bag is in my car."

Laura thought of her delicious expectations as she'd packed that overnight bag a few hours earlier. If she hadn't been so furious, she would have burst into tears, right on the spot. "You can mail it to me. I'll reimburse you for the postage."

Jason's hands closed over her shoulders and the feeling of his strong fingers on her bare skin electrified her. "I don't want to mail it to you." He leaned down and brushed his mouth against the silken creaminess of her neck. "I want you to come back inside with me, have dinner, and then go home with me, just like we planned."

"What about the taxi?" Her voice was breathless, her heart hammering in her ears.

He continued to nibble on her neck while his fingers kneaded her shoulders. "I'll leave a tip for the driver with the doorman, who can send him on his way."

She closed her eyes and leaned back against him. He slid one hand to her waist and closed his arm around her, holding her tightly. "The waiter will think we're crazy," Laura said breathlessly. "Running around as though we're practicing for a Chinese fire drill."

"Who cares? Come back with me, Laura." He sucked in his breath as his body reacted to the soft warmth of hers. "Please," he added.

"You said you wouldn't come after me," she whispered. "Why did you?"

"Because I couldn't *not* come after you," he said huskily. "I know, it makes no sense to me either."

Laura smiled and turned in his arms. "I'm glad you did, Jason." She slid her arms around his neck and feathered a string of light kisses along the curve of his jaw.

Jason groaned with pleasure. "Oh, baby, so am I."

Whatever their waiter's opinion of them, he kept it to himself and was deferential throughout the sumptuous dinner. And despite the inauspicious beginning, the evening proceeded like a romantic dream. The food was superb. Laura and Jason were attentive and absorbed in each other. They held hands and gazed raptly into each other's eyes and intertwined their legs under the table. They talked with the ease of good friends and the intimacy of lovers. And the passion burned between them with every look, every touch, every smile.

They left the restaurant shortly before ten, their arms around each other. And when they arrived at his condo, Jason scooped Laura up in his arms and carried her inside, so like a groom carrying his bride over the threshold that Laura's heart took flight.

He carried her into his bedroom and laid her down on the big bed. Laura sighed and clung to him, tracing the curve of his well-shaped mouth with her index finger. "It feels just like coming home," she murmured softly.

"Yes," Jason agreed, awed. "It feels exactly like that." He crushed her against him and buried his mouth in the hollow of her throat. "Lord, I've missed you, Laura. So much. It feels like I've been waiting years . . . to bring you home."

Their kisses were deep and passionate and ardently carnal. They discarded their clothes so quickly that they laughed at their own urgency. Then Jason's eyes swept over her hungrily. "I feel like I'm burning for you, Laura. I can't remember ever wanting anything as much as I want you."

"I want you to have me, Jason," she murmured, kissing him. "I want to give you whatever you want, whatever you need. Always." She would've liked to add that she loved him, but Lianna's reference to men's suspicion of the "L-word" restrained her. She didn't want him to feel pressured or manipulated, and she certainly didn't want to scare him with demands he didn't want to meet. She wanted him to know her love and need and desire for him.

Lovingly, she opened herself to him and he surged into her, joining them together in a masterful, timeless rhythm. Deeply in love, Laura cherished his possession of her and her own equally passionate possession of him. She gave herself to him, completely, without reserve, sharing in a boundless pleasure that strengthened the already powerful bonds between them. Their loving passion built and crested, sweeping them both to the shimmering, golden heights of rapture.

Ten

At ten o'clock on Sunday evening, Jason drove Laura from his condo back to her new apartment. It was a silent trip. Both were lost in memories of the weekend. They'd been inseparable, lovers and buddies. Laura remembered when Jason carried her to his outdoor hot tub after they'd made love on Saturday night. She'd never been in one before and she'd been surprised and delighted by the whirling warm water, lit by a myriad of tiny blue-and-white lights. They'd cuddled together, bathed by the swirling waves while the rain drizzled down on them. She sighed softly, savoring the sensual memory.

Jason glanced over at her and took her hand, laying it under his on his thigh. He smiled as he remembered her enthusiasm this afternoon when she'd unearthed a seldom-used badminton set in the outdoor storage shed. She'd helped him set up the net and they practiced a while before launching what Laura dubbed a world championship tournament. Laura was imaginative and fun to play with; she pretended that they were world-class players from rival nations competing to win the gold medal in badminton. Jason had enjoyed the fantasy as much as the game; he'd never had that kind of fun with a woman before.

And she'd been a terrific sport about him watching the Redskins play the Giants on TV at four o'clock. Though not particularly interested in the game herself, she read magazines and cooked dinner, which she served him in front of the television set. When he told her that he held season tickets for all the Redskins home games at RFK Stadium, she expressed the proper enthusiasm, without dropping obvious hints about him taking her to one. He usually took his friend Case Flynn along; if Case couldn't make it, he invited another guy. Jason was a firm believer in sports and male bonding, but for the first time he considered taking a woman to the next Redskins game. Laura.

He walked her to her apartment and saw her safely inside. "Jason, I—had a wonderful time," Laura said politely, suddenly shy with him. It seemed strange to have this wonderful weekend end like a conventional date after they'd been so close, so intimate.

He stared at her. She looked young and vulnerable and irresistibly appealing as she stood in this dingy cell masquerading as an apartment. How could he leave her here? "Yeah, I did too," he said gruffly, restraining the urge to pick her up and carry her away. Instead, he leaned down and kissed her forehead. "I'll see you tomorrow on Six-West."

She nodded and smiled brightly, giving him a little wave as he left. He sprinted down the three flights of stairs and dashed to his car, parked in the convenience store lot. Once inside, he stared up at the aging building for a long moment. And then he got out of the car, and raced across the street and back up the three flights of stairs to pound on Laura's door.

She opened it, her face registering both surprise and delight to see him there.

"Pack what you need for tonight and for work tomorrow," he ordered. "I'm not leaving you here. You're coming home with me."

Laura didn't argue. She hadn't wanted to leave him in the first place. It took her only a few minutes to gather up everything, including her uniform, shoes, and cap for tomorrow. They hurried down the steps, hand in hand, as if they were escaping, rather than simply leaving her apartment.

Dana, Zane, Beth, and some others that Laura didn't know but recognized from the Hospital Center were entering the building as Laura and Jason were leaving it.

Jason was holding Laura's suitcase in one hand and her hand with his other. Laura blushed as they exchanged greetings and good-byes within the space of a few seconds.

"Well, if there were any doubts about your involvement with me before, tonight puts them to rest," Jason remarked as he walked her to her car. Each had to have a car because of their different working hours. "We have eyewitnesses now to our involvement. Are you going to be able to handle the gossip, Laura?"

She smiled at him, her heart in her eyes. "I'm just happy to be with you, Jason," she said, her voice soft with love. "I don't care who knows about us—or who talks about us, either."

He tucked a strand of hair behind her ear in a loving, possessive gesture utterly foreign to the old Jason Fletcher. "I'll follow you back to my place. And drive carefully."

"Yes, Dr. Fletcher."

He grinned at her. "Could you inject just a little more subservience into your tone, nurse?"

Laughing, they climbed into their respective cars for the drive back to Jason's condominium.

Ms. Pecoraro, instructor with the diploma nursing school, arrived on Six-West with her eight students promptly at seven A.M. Laura nearly groaned at the sight of them. She hadn't discussed the possibility of assigning students to Jason's patients since that one unsuccessful attempt last week. Now Ms. Pecoraro was waiting expectantly, full of plans to assign the one male nursing student to young Terry Trice. It sounded like a good idea to Laura and she told the nursing instructor so. "But, of course, it all depends on Dr. Fletcher," she added.

"Here he comes now," Ms. Pecoraro said rather warily. "I think it would be best if *you* discussed this with him, Miss Novak. I'll just take the students into one of the examining rooms on the floor and look through the patient cardex with them."

Laura and Jason faced each other with a station full of interested bystanders looking on. They'd left his house separately this morning; the last time they'd been this close was when Jason had pulled her into the shower with him at five-thirty. Memories of that heated encounter enveloped them both.

"Hi," Jason said, striving to appear diffident and cool to their witnesses. His gray eyes told Laura a completely different story.

"Hi." She flushed. "Uh, Jason, Ms. Pecoraro and her students are here. She'd like to assign the male student to Terry Trice. He, that is, the student, is nineteen and loves football and she thought—we thought—that it would be a good experience for both Terry and the student." She smiled at him beneath her lashes, unconsciously flirting with him before she caught herself. Keeping Laura separate from Miss Novak, Head Nurse, was more difficult than she'd thought.

"My immediate inclination is to say no." It was Dr. Fletcher, not Jason, who stood before her, his expression stern. "I made a decision to keep my patients out of the clutches of the nursing schools. The other doctors didn't. There are plenty of orthopedic patients available for the nursing students."

SIMPLY IRRESISTIBLE • 163

"But Terry Trice is on *your* patient roster. Oh please, Jason! Remember what you told me about male bonding yesterday? Terry and this student could talk sports and—and whatever else males talk about while they're bonding . . ."

Jason smiled at her, his forbidding Dr. Fletcher mask melting away. She looked so earnest and sincere. He couldn't analyze his response to her; she was simply irresistible to him. "Well . . ." He shrugged. "I suppose Terry would appreciate the attention—and enjoy the company."

Laura's face was wreathed in smiles. "I'll find Ms. Pecoraro and tell her. She's keeping the students hidden in the examining room until your verdict," she added mischievously.

"Laura," he called after her. "You'll repeat to them that no carelessness will be tolerated on the part of any student or— "

"Of course. You're doing the right thing, Jason," Laura assured him fervently. "After all, it's hardly fair to hold every student responsible for the shortcomings of a very few in the past."

"No sermons, please," Jason said with mock severity. "And, um, Laura?"

She stepped closer to him. "Yes, Jason?" She wanted to slip her hand into his and lean up to kiss his cheek. It was hard not to follow her instincts and do just that.

"Are you going to your apartment when you get off work this afternoon?"

She nodded. "I thought I'd start painting the bathroom. The sickly green shade in there is hideous."

"Don't bother with it, honey. I'll pick you up around six-thirty."

There was no contest between painting a bilious green bathroom and being with Jason. Laura smiled her assent and hurried off to find Ms. Pecoraro.

•   •   •

September passed into October, the warmth of late summer giving way to crisp fall days, green leaves turning brilliant shades of red, yellow, and orange. Laura spent little time at her apartment. After a few days, she stopped returning there after work in the afternoons, going directly to Jason's luxurious condominium. She decided that living alone wasn't the only way to gain independence and courage and maturity; sharing a strong, satisfying relationship with the man she loved was just as effective. Soon, there were more of her things at Jason's than at her own place. They slept together, worked together, played together.

Some nights she cooked dinner for the two of them and some nights they went out to eat, sometimes alone, sometimes with other couples. Always married couples. It came as somewhat of a surprise to Jason to realize that he preferred the company of married couples over his bachelor cohorts and their dates. He and Laura seemed to have more in common with couples in established relationships than those indulging in silly dating games.

Occasionally, they took in a movie or a play, alone or with friends. He took her to the Redskins-Cowboys game at RFK Stadium and they had a good time, although both agreed that once was enough. Next game Jason would invite his pal Case and Laura would go shopping.

Aunt Sally and Uncle George invited them to Farview several times and Jason went without complaint. He found himself enjoying the way the older couple fussed over him and Laura; it was both amusing and endearing. He didn't bother to remember that not long ago, he would've considered his current existence intolerable, boring, and confining. With Laura at his side, he knew a peace and contentment he'd never before experienced. Or had wanted to.

The gossip which buzzed relentlessly about their

romance for the first few weeks lost its newsworthiness as time passed and they were still together. Besides, there was always newer, more exciting gossip to heat up the grapevine. The disclosure from the DEA lab that several of the Dilaudid vials which Jason had sent from 6-West had indeed been tampered with prompted an investigation throughout the hospital. The same problem—the narcotic replaced by saline solution—was found in vials taken from two other floors. Undercover investigators came into the hospital, and speculation ran high as to the identities of the agents and the culprit who'd stolen the drugs.

And late in October came the most spectacular piece of news, the breakup of Dana Shakarian and Zane Montrose, right in Terry Trice's room on Six-West. Terry's room had become a hangout for nursing students, both male and female, from all three schools. Since Zane Montrose was Terry's resident doctor, at first there seemed nothing suspicious in the fact that he often joined the student gatherings in the late afternoons and early evenings.

"I was always busy watching TV or talking with the other kids, Miss Novak," Terry told Laura and Jason shortly after the infamous happening, "and I didn't pay much attention to the fact that Dr. Montrose spent all his time talking and fooling around with Cassie Exton, one of the student nurses."

But word got back to Dana when Zane Montrose began seeing Cassie Exton outside of Terry's room. Cassie was spotted in Zane's apartment building and he was seen taking her to and from the student nurses' residence. On Halloween morning, Dana came to Terry's room to put him through an unscheduled series of range-of-motion exercises and was finishing up when Zane and Cassie walked in, laughing and holding hands.

"It was awesome, Miss Novak," Terry said as

Laura wrote up the incident report, in triplicate. "Dana just freaked. She grabbed the water pitcher and threw water all over Dr. Montrose. Cassie ran screaming out of the room and crashed into the aide bringing me my lunch tray, and food and dishes flew everywhere. Then Dr. Montrose tried to grab Dana and he slipped on some gravy, fell into the bedside table, and knocked over my radio. It fell into a puddle of water and shorted out. The sparks were flying."

Terry began to laugh. "I sure wish we could've gotten it on tape, Dr. Fletcher. It was better than a Three Stooges episode."

"Terrific. Exactly the sort of image we like to project here on orthopedics." Jason grimaced. "Serves Montrose right, the idiot! How did he expect Dana not to find out he's sneaking around on her when she's related to half the people working in this hospital? When her cousin lives in the same building as he does?"

"Poor Ms. Pecoraro is distraught," interjected Laura. "She's terrified you'll ban the students from your patients again, Jason. She said to tell you she's already lowered the Exton girl's grade one letter."

"Aw, that's not fair," said Terry. "It wasn't Cassie's fault. And you don't blame the students, do you, Dr. Fletcher? They're great!"

"No, I don't blame the students," said Jason. "They're doing a fine job. I guess I was—wrong to shut them out for so long." He smiled at Laura. "There, it wasn't as difficult to admit as I'd thought."

Laura returned his smile with an affection that melted him. And then she picked up the written copies of the mishap, listing the broken dishes, lost lunch, smashed radio, and bruised dietary aide. "I guess I'd better file this report now. I reads like a Three Stooges episode, all right." She rolled her eyes. "I shudder to think of the director of nursing—*Dana's cousin!*—reading this."

A group of students, nursing and medical, appeared at the door. "Terry, what happened in here?" exclaimed one of the girls. "You wouldn't believe the crazy rumors . . ."

"And they're all true," said Jason, taking Laura's arm to guide her from the room. "Fill them in, Terry." They left Terry holding court with his attentive audience.

"I can't understand Montrose—dumping a sweet girl like Dana." Jason scowled his disapproval as he and Laura walked down the corridor together. "And chasing after student nurses at his age! What a case of arrested development!"

Laura, who'd once heard Jason described in similar terms, hid a smile as he expressed his indignation and murmured her own sympathy for Dana.

Jason was still outraged the next night when he and Laura were having dinner with Sharla and Case Flynn at the Old Europe restaurant which specialized in German food.

"Poor Dana," Jason said, spearing a piece of his Wiener schnitzel with a blunt stab of his fork. "Everybody knows that she was crazy about Montrose. She committed herself to him, and he repays her by running around on her and then publicly humiliating her. It's just not right."

Sharla, Dana's cousin and Jason's longtime friend, regarded him with a wry smile. "I never thought I'd hear that from you, Jason. I thought you'd be defending Zane Montrose's timely escape from the—how did you used to describe it—'the suffocation of monogamy'?"

"Hey, we reformed rakes are virtual pillars of loyalty and commitment, right, Fletch?" Case said, grinning.

"If you don't make a commitment lightly, then you tend to take it very, very seriously when you finally do," Jason said thoughtfully.

"Well, we Shakarians don't make commitments

lightly," said Sharla, her dark eyes flaring. "Dan
was in love with Zane and everybody in the famil
is furious at the way he treated her."

"Someone ought to warn Montrose that he'
better watch his back," kidded Case. "The collec
tive Shakarian fury is an awesome sight to behold.

"I can understand why," Jason replied gravel
"Such a betrayal can only be taken seriously." H
reached over to take Laura's hand. Their gaze
met and held.

She saw the apprehension in his eyes, and i
that moment Laura understood that Jason's fur
wasn't exclusively on Dana's behalf. It was as
he'd finally acknowledged the depth of his ow
involvement with Laura and the enormous trus
he'd invested in her. Suddenly Jason Fletcher re
alized that he was vulnerable in ways he had neve
been before.

Laura squeezed his hand. Later that night, i
bed, she tried to prove how much she loved him
"I want you to be sure of me, Jason," she whis
pered as they lay together, sated in the swee
aftermath of their passion. "I'll never, ever inten
tionally do anything to hurt you."

"Of course you won't, sweetheart." Jason kisse
her lazily. After the hot, sweet intensity of thei
lovemaking, he felt powerful and confident, a ma
who knows he is loved by his woman, who know
he can satisfy his woman. It was a heady, sex
triumph and he reveled in it. "I know how mucl
you love me," he added. He didn't bother to ad
that he loved her too; he hadn't quite worked tha
out yet.

Jason Fletcher, sophisticated, spoiled, and ex
perienced, was still very much a novice in th
arena of love.

The Sports Medicine Orthopedic Conference wa
scheduled to be held in Houston in the middle o

November. "I wish you were coming with me," Jason said to Laura as she helped him pack the night before he was to leave. He stared at the conference brochure which listed the program of activities for the spouses accompanying their doctor husbands and wives to the conference. He frowned. "I already told you, I'll pay for your plane fare, for everything, Laura."

"I'd have to take off Tuesday through Friday, and I haven't earned that much vacation time yet." She carefully folded his shirts and placed them into the suitcase. "I'm going to miss you, Jason," she added softly. It would be their first separation and she hated the prospect.

"Oh, baby." Jason pulled her into his arms. "I'll miss you too." He heaved a groan. "I signed up for this conference back in March, way before I met you, and now I'm stuck with it."

Way back in March, he'd anticipated a four-day romp in Houston along with the professional advantages of the conference. Now the idea of romping was repellent to him; he already knew that this was the first conference where he wasn't going to miss a single seminar.

It was a sad good-bye. Saturday, the day of his return, seemed light years away. Laura cried when Jason drove away to the airport. The condo seemed intolerably empty without him. She considered driving to Farview and spending the rest of the week with Aunt Sally and Uncle George, but dismissed the idea. Lianna had recently moved into her own apartment in the District; this was the first time in twenty years that Aunt Sally and Uncle George had their home to themselves. Though she knew they would welcome her with open arms, Laura decided that they deserved a break from parenting the Novaks.

Besides, she had her own apartment . . . The idea of spending the rest of this lonely week there appealed to her at once. She wouldn't have to bear the loneliness of Jason's place without Jason in it. There were lots of people she knew in the apartment building; she'd had lunch in the hospital cafeteria several times with Beth Shakarian and her roommate Sarah. She could visit with Beth and Sarah. Maybe they would want to go to dinner or a movie one evening.

She knew she'd made the right decision when she arrived at Beth and Sarah's door later that night and they immediately invited her in and insisted that she join them in watching a sexy romantic movie on their VCR. Two young nurses from across the hall joined them and Beth made popcorn, and they all stayed long after the movie ended, laughing and talking late into the night.

She had lunch with Dana, Beth, and Sarah in the hospital cafeteria the next day and they made plans to go to a nearby shopping mall together after work. Laura had just arrived back on Six-West when the ward clerk handed her the phone. "Long distance call for you, Miss Novak."

"Jason!" Laura exclaimed happily when she heard his voice.

"Where in the hell have you been?" Jason barked across the line. "I called you yesterday when I got to the hotel and there was no answer for hours. I finally gave up and went to bed."

Laura told him of her decision to spend the week at her apartment and the impromptu get-together at Beth's apartment. "I haven't spent an evening with a bunch of girls since nursing school," she added, smiling. "It was sort of like an old-fashioned pajama party. We had such a good time."

"So while I was going out of my mind worrying about you, you were yukking it up with the girls." Jason sounded decidedly petulant.

Laura glanced around at the normal hectic midday clamor of the nurses' station. It was not a good time or place to be having this conversation.

"Jason, will you give me your telephone number and I'll call you tonight?" she asked, quickly reaching for a pencil to scribble it down.

"Are you sure you can fit it into your busy social life?" Jason was not pleased that she seemed to be thriving without him. He was miserable without her. All he could think about was how much he missed her and how glad he would be to get home to her. And she was running around like a giddy student nurse, not missing him at all!

After spending several hours at the mall, Laura, Dana, Beth, and Sarah went to dinner at a dilapidated spaghetti house which served the best pasta Laura had ever tasted. She told Jason about it when she called him later that night. "We have to go there when you get back, Jason. You'll love it."

"I'm sure I will." He wanted her to tell him how lost and lonely she was without him. Then maybe— *maybe*—he could say something similar to her.

But Laura considered it her duty to sound upbeat long distance, on the theory that being apart was hard enough and there was nothing to be gained by telephone-induced depression. She hung up, happy to have heard the sound of his voice and very much in love. He hung up, feeling isolated and fighting a sickening feeling that she was drifting away from him, that he was losing her.

A grand master when it came to sex, he was an anxious novice in the art of love.

Eleven

On Friday night the intern who lived three doors down the hall from Laura threw a party. Everybody in the building was invited, and Beth and Sarah talked Laura into going along with them. She had half a beer and a piece of pizza and talked for awhile, but when the lights were lowered and the dancing began, she knew it was time for her to go. This was a party for singles and she—well, she didn't feel single. She watched the couples pair off and sway to the music and felt an acute pang of loneliness. It seemed so long since she'd last been with Jason; she missed him terribly.

She had so much to tell him about the things she had done while he was away, about all the goings-on at the Hospital Center. She couldn't wait to tell him that an orderly, one who "floated" between three floors including Six-West, had been caught trying to steal narcotics on Four-West during the night shift! The investigator, working undercover as a janitor, had apprehended the orderly as he was siphoning the narcotic from the vial. The saline replacement had been right there too, just as Jason had guessed. Laura couldn't wait to tell him how proud she was of his perceptive theorizing.

She tried to cheer herself up by reminding herself that he would be home tomorrow, but it didn't help much. She wanted him there now; she was aching for him in every possible way there was for her to ache. She was so in love with him. Tomorrow felt as far away as the Fourth of July.

She returned to her apartment and slipped on her knee-length pink cotton nightshirt, a gift from one of her cousins, the type of sleeping apparel she no longer wore. She bought silky, sexy nightgowns to wear for Jason or she wore nothing at all. Laura felt heat surge through her as her mind played back a visual retrospective of the nights she spent with Jason. And tomorrow, tomorrow . . .

She poured herself a glass of cold orange juice to cool down her fevered body.

After watching the eleven o'clock news on television—they'd carried the story of the orderly's arrest—she tried to go to bed. But the noise from the party down the hall made sleeping an impossibility. Sighing, Laura put on some of her own records, wrapped herself in the afghan Aunt Sally had crocheted for her, curled up on the couch, and tried to read.

It was nearly midnight when the pounding on her door began. She was astonished to find Zane Montrose, clad only in a pair of white running shorts, standing outside. He reeked of alcohol and her first instinct was to quickly close the door.

He must've sensed it. "No, Laura, please, don't shut me out, I've already had the door slammed in my face three times tonight. First by Dana over at her place, then by Beth and by Sarah here. Laura, I have to talk to someone or I'll go crazy!"

Laura scowled at him. "Why don't you go talk to Cassie Exton, then? You remember her, the little tart you dumped Dana for?"

To her incredulity, Zane began to cry. "Oh, Laura, it was the biggest mistake of my life. I don't know why I did it. I—I love Dana. I just never realized it until I lost her."

Laura heaved a sigh. "Come in, Zane. I'll make you some coffee."

He stumbed into the room and flopped down on the couch. "I was such a macho big shot, Laura. I knew how much Dana liked me from the very beginning. I took it for granted, and when she fell in love with me, I took that for granted too. When Cassie started flirting with me, I—"

"Zane, if you're going to say that you were seduced by a teenage Jezebel, I'm not going to believe you. You're a lot older than Cassie. You're more responsible for seducing her. And where are your shirt and your shoes? It's the middle of November, for heaven's sake! It's forty degrees outside."

"I know. I don't care. After Dana refused to see me tonight, I decided to go jogging."

"And so you took off your shirt and your shoes? What did you have in mind, suicide by jogging?"

He began to shiver and pulled Laura's colorful afghan around him. "Laura, I love Dana. I have to get her back. Tell me what I can do—I'll do anything!" He began to sob.

Laura felt rather sorry for him. He hadn't valued Dana's love and from what she'd heard from Dana and other Shakarians, he didn't stand a snowball's chance in hell of winning it back.

But she didn't tell him so. It was late and he was half drunk and cold and miserable. She sat with him while he drank the coffee and poured out his heart about his lost love.

"I'd make Dana so happy, Laura. Happier than she was before, when I was an arrogant, self-satisfied son of a bitch who took her love as my due." Zane took Laura's hand and clung to it like a drowning victim clutches the life preserver thrown to him. "But she won't give me the chance,

Laura. I'm scared she really doesn't want me anymore."

A reasonable assumption, Laura thought but didn't say. "Zane, I think that you—" she began but never had the chance to finish because her apartment door opened and Jason, wearing a blue three-piece suit, yellow shirt, and foulard tie, strode in.

His eyes swept over the small room, taking in the soft music, the lateness of the hour, and the couple's attire as they lounged on the sofa. Laura, in a sexy nightshirt—for he considered her sexy in anything she wore—and Zane Montrose in white underpants, a blanket loosely draped over them. The smell of alcohol pervaded the room. He stood there staring, thunderstruck at the scene.

"Jason!" Laura jumped to her feet. "I thought you weren't coming home until tomorrow." She started to run to him, but the chilling, forbidding expression on his face halted her in her tracks.

"Obviously," he said in a cold, cruel tone she had never heard him use before.

He left the apartment and headed for the stairs, pale and shaken and so furious he could barely think. He'd left the conference early, skipping the final banquet tonight because he couldn't stand to be away from Laura any longer. All during the monotonous flight from Houston, he'd thought of their reunion, picturing her surprise and delight when she saw him at her door.

He'd surprised her all right. Drinking and making love with Zane Montrose! A searing agony tore through him and he ran down the steps, taking them three at a time. He had to get out of there, he had to get away . . . his pain-wracked brain could formulate no plans or thoughts after that.

He'd left his car in the parking lot of the convenience store across the street and he was climbing into it when he heard his name.

"Jason!" cried Laura, running out of the apartment building and into the street. She had chased after him, not bothering to pull on a robe or slippers. "Jason, wait! Please!"

"Go back to your new lover!" Jason shouted back at her. She was a faithless, heartless little bitch who'd been having the time of her life this week while he'd been missing her, loving her . . .

Laura almost made it to the car. "Jason, you can't honestly believe that Zane and I—"

"I saw you with my own eyes!" he interrupted, his face a savage mask of fury and betrayal. A spasm of pain, the force of which he'd never known, ripped through him. "You and Montrose deserve each other!" he added, slamming the door and gunning the engine. Zane Montrose, who'd cheated on Dana, who'd betrayed her trust after she'd given him all her love . . . and Laura, who'd done exactly the same thing to him! Oh, yes, that pair of lying deceivers belonged together.

He sped off into the night, the tires squealing. Laura stood in the parking lot, so numb that she wasn't even aware of the cold pavement beneath her bare feet or the stiff night wind that whipped through her hair and the pink cotton of her nightshirt. So stunned with shock and pain that she didn't notice the three punks, in their late teens or early twenties, approaching her. Not until they surrounded her.

Jason was perspiring, his heart thundering in his chest and echoing in his eardrums; his stomach roiled with nausea. He drove two, three, four blocks in that condition until a red light forced him to brake to a stop. And as he sat there in his car, the engine idling, his first coherent thought since he'd set foot in Laura's apartment managed to filter through the morass of his mind.

He was going home alone. The realization nearly set off another torrent of pain-crazed wildness. But the light was still red and he couldn't go anywhere and he thought of how he'd planned to take Laura back to the condo with him, to tell her how much he'd missed her, how much he loved her. Yes, he had finally realized that he was deeply, passionately, irrevocably in love for the first time in his life.

And he'd returned to find her in the arms of another man. Jason flinched. Laura didn't love him.

It was then that some modicum of sanity returned. *Laura didn't love him?* Ridiculous! The emotional fog slowly began to lift, enabling him to think clearly again. She'd spent the past two and a half months doing everything in her power to show him just how much she really did love him. Everything she said, everything she did . . . He wasn't stupid and she was not an actress. They hadn't been living a lie these past months. Laura loved him. Incredibly, he wondered how he could have doubted it for even a moment.

The acknowledgement forced him to reconsider what he'd seen tonight. Or what he *thought* he'd seen. Everything he knew about Laura, from the many hours they'd spent together, from what he'd gleaned about her from her family and friends and coworkers, did not add up to a Laura who would take advantage of the week-long absence of the man she loved to indulge in a boozy fling with another man.

And Zane Montrose? Why, if Laura really wanted him, she could've had him months ago. Except she hadn't wanted him. Ever. The only man she wanted was Jason Fletcher, her first and only lover.

The man who'd just displayed an appalling lack of faith and trust in her, who'd run off leaving her standing cold and alone in a parking lot. The image of Laura, ashen and shivering, calling his name, flashed before his mind's eye like the thrust of a knife blade.

The light turned green and Jason took advan-

178 • BARBARA BOSWELL

tage of the lack of cars in the street to make a
U-turn and head back in the opposite direction.
To Laura.

He made it back to the store in record time. His
mind was so preoccupied with thoughts of Laura
that he hardly noticed the trio of young men,
gathered in a circle along the dark side of the
store. It was the flash of pink from within that
circle that made him focus on the scene.

His heart seemed to crash to a stop and then
start again at a manic pace. It was Laura, bare-
foot and in her nightshirt, who was being held
prisoner by the trio.

Jason rolled down his window and drove over
the curb. "Get away from her, you punks!" he
shouted, his voice sounding threatening and mur-
derous, even to his own ears. The sight of them
terrorizing Laura evoked a primitive rage. "Or I'll
run you down." He was prepared to do it; he even
welcomed the opportunity. Speeding up, he pointed
the car toward them and headed directly for them.

The punks yelled and cursed and jumped out of
the way, scattering into the night.

"Laura, get in the car," Jason called.

Laura stood against the cold bricks of the wall,
her eyes huge in her white, white face. She was
beyond tears, too numbed by heartbreak and terror to cry. Or even to feel relief when Jason reap-
peared and chased off the thugs.

She felt his arms around her and then he was
picking her up and carrying her to the car, where
he dropped her into the passenger seat and then
climbed behind the wheel.

They sped away, Laura staring straight ahead,
the city lights blurring before her.

"Laura, are you all right?" Jason demanded
hoarsely. "Did they hurt you?" Wrath boiled within
him with volcanic force. He wanted to pound on
those punks for daring to come near her. And he

was enraged with himself for subjecting her to such danger.

"They—They were just—s-saying things." Her throat was almost too dry to speak. The words sounded more like squeaky croaks. "They didn't touch me." She closed her eyes, remembering their obscene threats. "Yet."

She began to shiver, from reaction, from the cold. Her teeth chattered and she couldn't make them stop. Jason pulled over to the side of the road and took off his suit jacket. He wrapped it around her, then pulled her into his arms.

"Oh, God, Laura, can you ever forgive me?" He rocked her in his arms until he felt her stop shaking. "I love you, darling. I adore you. When I saw you in danger back there—"

She closed her eyes and relaxed against him, feeling his warmth and strength replace the terrible chill that had pervaded her body and heart and soul. "Jason, I wasn't with Zane tonight," she whispered, drawing back a little to gaze up at him. "Not the way you think. You see, he realized that he still loves Dana and—"

"No, sweetheart, you don't have to explain. I trust you, I believe in you. And I despise myself for doubting you tonight. Laura, I'll do anything to make it up to you if you'll just let me." His arms tightened and he crushed her fiercely against him. "Darling, you have to let me!"

The pain and terror had abated enough to permit her to manage a shaky smile. "I'll let you, Jason." He was here with her, he loved her, and everything was going to be all right! She felt lightheaded with relief and lighthearted with joy. "What did you have in mind?" she asked tremulously.

His eyes grew moist. "Laura, I don't deserve you."

She cuddled closer, lifting her mouth to his. She brushed her lips over his, lightly, enticingly. "Of course you do. You're Jason Fletcher and you always get everything you want. And if you want me—"

"I want you." He slipped his hand between the lapels of the jacket and ran his palm slowly, amorously over her breast. His thumb traced the taut outline of her nipple beneath the cloth, and Laura went soft and hot and weak.

"Then I'm yours," she whispered.

"Sweetheart, this isn't the time or the place for the romantic proposal I had in mind, but I don't want to waste a single moment more. Will you marry me, Laura?" His mouth covered hers for a slow, deep kiss.

Laura lay in his arms, feeling safe and warm and loved. "Oh yes, Jason. I love you so much." She smiled up at him, her face alight with joy and love. "But then, you've known that for a long time, haven't you?"

Jason gazed tenderly at her. "Yes, love. And I've loved you for a long time too."

She arched her brows and he nodded insistently. "It's true, Laura. I was just too—stupid? stubborn? *inexperienced?*—to realize it. I might've been a professional swinging bachelor but I'm a rank amateur when it comes to being a man in love. You'll be patient with me, I hope?"

"I think you're a wonderful man in love, Jason. A wonderful man to love. And yes, I'll marry you, my love. Whenever you want."

"Whenever *you* want," he corrected gently. "We'll have whatever kind of wedding you want, Laura. And the sooner the better. I'm very eager to become your husband."

She smiled. "And I can't wait to be your wife." She thought of that big white wedding she had planned with Danny, which had ended in tragedy, and decided that this wedding must be totally different. She wanted no sad reminders of the past. Her life with Jason was a whole new beginning for them both. "I think I'd like a private ceremony with just our families, Jason."

"Is next weekend too soon for you, honey?"

"Next weekend is perfect for me, Jason."

They kissed lingeringly one last time before Jason started the car again to resume their drive home. He carried her into the house, exactly like a newly engaged man would.

Laura was puzzled when he set her down on the sofa instead of carrying her straight to bed. "I'll be back in a minute, darling," he promised and returned shortly wearing a red flannel robe, obviously brand-new, and a thick pair of white sweat socks. He was carrying a matching robe and socks.

"Are you still cold, sweetie?" he asked, slipping her arms into the sleeves of the robe. It was too big for her, but he pulled it around her and belted it, then put the socks on her feet.

"Jason?" Laura was laughing. "What are you doing? Where did these robes and socks come from?"

"I bought them in Houston for us. A matching set, for those evenings at home in front of the TV." He sat down beside her and pulled her onto his lap. "Humor me. It's a fantasy I've had for a long time."

"I'm always glad to play a role in your fantasies," she murmured, gazing up at him with wide, flirtatious eyes.

He traced her mouth with his thumb. "I love you, Laura. And I want our marriage to be the kind you described that night at the Jean-Louis. I want to give you everything—my name, my children, all that I have. I want you to have all of me and I want all of you." He smiled. "No stingy little parcels of ourselves for us."

"Never." Laura sighed, melting into him, loving him more than anyone else in the world ever could or would. She had never been happier. She was home with the man she loved, the man she was going to marry, the man whose babies she would carry.

"You're perfect for me," Jason said huskily, tenderly. "Simply irresistible. I think I knew from the time you caught that ball in the hospital picnic softball game that you were the one for me."

"I think so too," agreed Laura as they lovingly revised their history. Their children would hear the story of love at first sight on the softball field. But all of that would come later. For now, they wanted to celebrate their good fortune in finding each other, in loving each other.

Slowly, their mouths touched and tasted and tantalized before coming together with a kiss of love and commitment, of passion and bliss and belonging.

THE EDITOR'S CORNER

Next month we kick off one of LOVESWEPT's most sizzling summers! First, we bring you just what you've been asking for—

•

LOVESWEPT GOLDEN CLASSICS

•

We are ushering in this exciting program with four of the titles you've most requested by four of your most beloved authors . . .

•

Iris Johansen's
THE TRUSTWORTHY REDHEAD
(Originally published as LOVESWEPT #35)

•

Billie Green's
TEMPORARY ANGEL
(Originally published as LOVESWEPT #38)

•

Fayrene Preston's
THAT OLD FEELING
(Originally published as LOVESWEPT #45)

•

Kay Hooper's
SOMETHING DIFFERENT
(Originally published as LOVESWEPT #46)

With stunning covers—richly colored, beautifully enhanced by the golden signatures of the authors—LOVESWEPT'S GOLDEN CLASSICS are pure pleasure for those of you who missed them five years ago and exquisite "keepers" for the libraries of those who read and loved them when they were first published. Make sure your bookseller holds a set just for you or order the CLASSICS through our LOVESWEPT mail order subscription service.

And now a peek at our six new sensational romances for next month.

We start off with the phenomenal Sandra Brown's **TEMPER-ATURES RISING**, LOVESWEPT #336. Handsome Scout Ritland is celebrating the opening of a hotel he helped build on a lush South Pacific island when he's lured into a garden by an extraordinarily beautiful woman. But Chantal duPont has more in
(continued)

mind than a romantic interlude on this sultry moonlit night. She wants Scout all right—but to build a bridge, a bridge to connect the island on which she grew up with the mainland. Then there's an accident that Chantal never intended and that keeps Scout her bedridden patient. In the shadow of an active volcano the two discover their fierce hunger for each other . . . and the smoldering passion between them soon explodes with far-reaching consequences. This is Sandra Brown at her best in a love story to cherish. And remember—this wonderful romance is also available in a Doubleday hardcover edition.

Since bursting onto the romance scene with her enormously popular **ALL'S FAIR** (remember the Kissing Bandit?), Linda Cajio has delighted readers with her clever and sensual stories. Here comes an especially enchanting one, **DESPERATE MEASURES,** LOVESWEPT #337. Ellen Kitteridge is an elegant beauty who draws Joe Carlini to her as iron draws a magnet. Wild, virile, Joe pursues her relentlessly. Ellen is terrified because of her early loveless marriage to a treacherous fortune hunter. She runs from Joe, hides from him . . . but she can't escape. And Joe is determined to convince her that her shattered past has nothing to do with their thrilling future together. Linda's **DESPERATE MEASURES** will leave you breathless!

That brilliant new star of romance writing Deborah Smith gives you another thrilling story in *The Cherokee Trilogy,* **TEMPTING THE WOLF,** LOVESWEPT #338. This is the unforgettable tale of a brilliant, maverick Cherokee who was a pro football player and is now a businessman. Of most concern to Erica Gallatin, however, is his total (and threatening) masculinity. James is dangerous, perfection molded in bronze, absolutely irresistible—and he doesn't trust beautiful "non-Indian" women one bit! Erica is determined to get in touch with her heritage as she explores the mystery of Dove's legacy . . . and she's even more determined to subdue her mad attraction to the fierce warrior who is stealing her soul. This is a romance as heart-warming as it is heart-stopping in its intensity.

Judy Gill produces some of the most sensitive love stories we publish. In LOVESWEPT #339, **A SCENT OF ROSES,** she will once again capture your emotions with the exquisite romance of a memorable hero and heroine. Greg Miller is a race car driver who's lost his memory in an accident. His wife, Susan, puts past hurts aside when she agrees to help him recover. At his family's home in the San Juan Islands—a setting made for love—they rediscover the passion they shared . . . but can they

(continued)

compromise on the future? A thrilling story of deep passion and deep commitment nearly destroyed by misunderstanding.

It's always our greatest pleasure to discover and present a brand-new talent. Please give a warm, warm welcome to Courtney Henke, debuting next month with **CHAMELEON**, LOVESWEPT #340. This is a humorous yet emotionally touching romance we suspect you will never forget . . . in large measure because of its remarkable hero. Emma Machlen is a woman with a single purpose when she invades Maxwell Morgan's domain. She's going to convince the cosmetics mogul to buy the unique fragrance her family has developed. She's utterly desperate to make the sale. But she never counts on the surprises Max will have for her, not the least of which is his incredible attractiveness. Enchanted by Emma, drawn to her against his will, Max is turned upside down by this little lady whom he *must* resist. Emma has her work cut out for her in winning over Max . . . but the poor man never has a chance! An absolutely wonderful story!

And what could make for more sizzling reading than another of Helen Mittermeyer's Men of Fire? Nothing I can think of. All the passion, intensity, emotional complexity, richness, and humor you expect in one of Helen's love stories is here in **WHITE HEAT**, LOVESWEPT #341. When Pacer Dillon—that irresistible heartbreaker Helen introduced you to before—meets Colm Fitzroy, he is dead set on taking over her family business. She's dead set on stopping him. Irresistible force meets immovable object. Colm is threatened now, having been betrayed in the past, and Pacer is just the man to save her while using the sweet, hot fire of his undying love to persuade her to surrender her heart to him. Pure dynamite!

Enjoy all our LOVESWEPTs—new and old—next month! And please remember that we love to hear from you.

Sincerely,

Carolyn Nichols

Carolyn Nichols
Editor
LOVESWEPT
Bantam Books
666 Fifth Avenue
New York, NY 10103